A Friend In Need

★ ★ ★ ★ ★

I sat down near the window, and lighted a cigar. Luane Devore sniffed distastefully, and I sniffed right back at her. "All right," I said. "Let's get it over with. What's the matter now?"

Her mouth worked. She took a grayish handkerchief from beneath her pillow, and blew into it. "It—it's R-Ralph, Kossy. He's planning to kill me!"

"Yeah?" I said. "So what's wrong with that?"

"He is, Kossy! I know you don't believe me, but he is!"

"Swell," I said. "You tell him if he needs any help just to give me a ring."

Also by Jim Thompson

NOVELS

Now and On Earth • Heed the Thunder
Nothing More Than Murder
Cropper's Cabin • The Killer Inside Me
The Alcoholics • Bad Boy* • The Criminal
Recoil • Savage Night • A Swell-Looking Babe
The Ripoff* • The Golden Gizmo*
A Hell of a Woman • The Nothing Man*
Roughneck* • After Dark, My Sweet
Wild Town • The Getaway • The Transgressors
The Grifters • Pop. 1280 • Texas by the Tail
Ironside (novelization of TV series) • South of Heaven
The Undefeated (novelization of screenplay)
Nothing But a Man (novelization of screenplay)
Child of Rage • King Blood

*Forthcoming from
THE MYSTERIOUS PRESS

THE KILL-OFF

JIM THOMPSON

THE MYSTERIOUS PRESS

New York • London

I

Kossmeyer

MOSTLY, SHE WAS a woman who loved scandal—and lived by it.

Luane Devore made a specialty of being impetuous, bold, headstrong and—she thought—sultry.

Mostly, though . . . It was Sunday, only two days after the season had opened, when Luane Devore telephoned. As usual, she sounded a little hysterical. As usual, she was confronted with a dire emergency which only I could handle. Significantly, however—or at least I thought it significant —she did not calm down when I told her to go to hell, and to stop acting like a damned fool.

"Please, Kossy," she burbled. "You must come! It's vitally important, darling. I can't talk about it over the telephone, but—"

"Why the hell can't you?" I cut in. "You talk about everything and everyone else over the phone. Now, lay off, Luane. I'm a lawyer, not a baby-sitter. I'm here on a vacation, and I'm not going to spend all my time listening to you moan and whine about a lot of imaginary problems."

She wept audibly. I felt a very small twinge of conscience. The Devore estate didn't amount to anything any more. It had been years since I'd gotten a nickel out of her. So... well, you see what I mean. When people don't have anything—when they can't do anything for you—you kind of have to go a little easy on 'em.

"Now, take it easy, honey," I said. "Be a big girl for Kossy. The world ain't going to come to an end if I don't dash up there right now. It ain't going to kill you, is it?"

"Yes," she said. "Yes, it is!" And then she hung up with a wild sob.

I hung up also. I came out of the bedroom, crossed the living room and returned to the kitchen. Rosa was at the stove, her back turned to me. She was talking, ostensibly mumbling to herself but actually addressing me. It is a habit of hers, one she has resorted to more and more frequently during the twenty-odd years of our marriage. I listened to the familiar words ... *bum* ... *loafer* ... *time-waster* ... *thinks-nothing-of-his-wife-but* ... and for the first time in a long time I was affected by them. I began to get sore—angry and sad. And a little sick on the inside.

"So I'm sorry," I said. "She's a client. She's in trouble. I've got no choice but to see her."

"A client, he says," Rosa said. "So, of course, everything else he must drop. She is his only client, is she not? His first case?"

"With a good lawyer," I said, "it is always the first case. Don't make such a production out of it, dammit. I'll be back in a little while."

"In a little while, he says," Rosa said. "In a little while, he was going to help with the unpacking. He was going to help clean up the cottage, and take his wife bathing and—"

"I will," I said. "Goddammit, you want me to put it in writing?"

"Listen to him," she said. "Listen to the great attorney curse at his wife. See how he acts, the great attorney, when it is his wife he deals with."

"Listen to yourself," I said. "See how you act."

She turned around unwillingly. I stood up and put on a performance, watching her face slowly turn red then white. I am pretty good at such mimicry. Painfully good, you might say. I have a talent for it; and when a man is only five feet tall, when he has had no formal law education—damned little formal education of any kind—he leaves no talent undeveloped.

"This is you," I said. "Mrs. Abie. Why don't you go on TV? Go into vaudeville? They love those characters."

"N-now—" she smiled weakly. "I guess I'm not that bad, Mister Smarty."

"Mister Smarty," I said. "Now, there's a good line. You just keep it up, keep building on that stuff, and we'll be all fixed up. We'll be getting a nice offer for our property."

"Maybe," she snapped, "we'd better not wait for an offer. If you're ashamed of your own wife, if you're so worried about what your friends may think of me—"

"What I'm ashamed of is someone that isn't my wife. This character you've slipped into. Goddammit, you're supposed to amount to something, and yet half the time you—"

I stopped myself short.

She said, "Listen to him, listen to the great attorney..." And then she caught herself.

We stood staring at each other. After a long moment, I started to break the silence; and the first word was a swear word and the second one was an ain't. I broke off again. "Look at who's talking," I said. "Me, telling you how to behave!"

She laughed and put her arms around me, and I put mine around her. "But you're right, darling," she murmured. "I don't know how I ever got into the habit of carrying on that way. You stop me if I do it any more."

"And you stop me," I said.

She warmed up the breakfast coffee, and we both had a cup. Chatting and smoking a cigarette while we drank it. Then, I got the car out of the garage, and headed up the beach road toward town.

* * *

Manduwoc is a seacoast town, a few hours train-ride from New York City. It is too far from the city for commuting; there are no local industries. According to the last census, the population was 1,280 and I doubt that it has increased since then.

It used to be quite a resort town, back before the war, but the number of summer visitors has declined steadily in recent years. The natives got a little too independent; they leaned a little too heavily on the gypping. So, what with so many places closer to the population centers, Manduwoc began to go downhill.

The largest hotel here has been boarded up for the past two summers. Some business establishments have closed down permanently; and at least a third of the beach cottages are never rented. There is still a considerable influx of vacationers, but nothing like there used to be. Practically the only people who come here now are those who own property here. People who, generally speaking, are out to save money rather than spend it.

The town proper sits a few hundred yards back from the ocean. Built around a courthouse square, it is adjoined, on the land side, by an area of summer estates, and, on the sea side, by the usual resort installations. These last include the aforementioned hotels and cottages, a couple of seafood restaurants, a boat-and-bait concession, a dance pavilion and so on.

Our cottage, which we own, is about three miles out. The others—the rent-cottages, I should say—are all close-in. I was approaching them, row upon row of identical clapboard structures, when a man stepped out onto the road and began to trudge toward the village. He was tall, stoop-shouldered, very thin. He had a mop of gray-black hair, and his angular, intelligent face was almost a dead white.

I pulled the car even with him and stopped. He went on walking, looking straight ahead. I called to him, "Rags! Rags McGuire!" And, finally, after another hail or two, he turned around.

He was frowning, in a kind of fiercely absent way. He came toward me slowly, his features twisted in that vacant scowl. And, then, suddenly, his face lit up with a smile of friendliness and recognition.

"Kossy! How are you, boy?" He climbed into the seat with me. "Where you been hiding yourself?"

I said that Rosa and I were just getting settled down; we'd be dropping by the pavilion as soon as we were finished. He beamed and slapped me on the back, and said that was the Kossy kid. And then he went completely silent. It wasn't an awkward silence. Not seemingly, that is, on his part. But there was something about it, something about his smile—and his eyes—that made me more ill at ease than I have ever been in my life.

"I don't suppose—" I hesitated. "I mean, is Janie with the band this summer?"

He didn't say anything for several seconds. Then, he said no, she wasn't with him. He had a new vocalist. Janie was staying in the city with the kids.

"I figure that gives her enough to do," he added. "Just bringing the kids up right, y'know. After all, you take a couple of boys that age, and a woman don't have time to— Yeah? You were saying, Kossy?"

"Nothing," I said. "I mean—well, the boys are all right, then?"

"All right?" He looked bewildered for a moment. Then, he laughed amiably. "Oh, I guess you saw that little story in the papers, huh? Well, that wasn't Janie. That wasn't my family."

"I see," I said. "I'm certainly glad to hear it, Rags."

"Ain't it hell, though?" he said musingly. "A guy wants some publicity—he knocks himself out to get some—and he just can't swing it. But let something phony come along, something that won't do him no good, y'know, and he'll make the papers every time."

"Yeah," I said. "That's the way it seems to go, all right."

"I thought about suing them," he said. "But then I thought, what the hell? After all, it was a natural mistake. It

was the same name—names—see? And Janie does have a
rep for tipping the bottle."

I was almost convinced. In fact, I'm not at all sure that I
wasn't. There were probably any number of small-time band
leaders named McGuire. It would be easy to confuse one
with another, particularly in a case where a story had to be
written largely from newspaper files. And that had been the
case in this instance. The two boys had died in the crash.
Janie—if it *was* Janie—had lived, but she had been in a
coma for days.

Rags had me drop him off in front of a bar. I drove on
through town, wondering, worrying, then mentally shrug-
ging. He wasn't a close friend—not a friend at all, really.
Just a guy I'd got to know during the summers I'd come
here. I liked him, like I like a lot of people. But he wasn't
my business. Luane Devore was; and straightening her out
would be headache enough for one day.

She lived in a two-story, brick box of a house on the
land-side outskirts of Manduwoc. It sat a few hundred feet
back from the road, at the apex of a wooded slope. The
driveway curved up through an expanse of meticulously
clipped, lushly green lawn; in the rear of the house, there
was more lawn, stretching out fan-wise to the whitewashed
gates and fences of the orchard, barnyard and pasture. I
parked my car beneath the portecochere and took a quick
glance around the place.

A sleek Jersey grazed in the pasture. Several dozen Leg-
horns scratched and pecked industriously in the barnyard. A
sow and half a dozen piglets wandered through the orchard,
grunting and squealing contentedly as they gobbled the
fallen fruit. Everything was as I remembered it from last
season. Over all there was an air of peace and contentment,
the evidence of loving care, of quiet pride in homely accom-
plishments.

You don't find that much any more—that kind of pride, I
mean. People who will give everything they have to a humble, run-of-the-mill job. At the office boys want to be company presidents. All the store clerks want to be department

heads. All the waitresses and waiters want to be any damned thing but what they are. And they all let you know it—the whole lazy, shiftless, indifferent, insolent lot. They can't do their own jobs well; rather, they won't do them. But, by God, they're going to have something better—the best! They're going to have it or else, and meanwhile it's a case of do as little as you can and grab as much as you can get.

So I stood there in the drive, looking around and feeling better the longer I looked. And, then, from an upstairs window, Luane Devore called down to me petulantly.

"Kossy? *Kossy!* What are you doing down there?"

"I'll be right up," I said. "Is the door unlocked?"

"Of course it's unlocked! It's always unlocked! You know that! How in the world could I—"

"Save it," I said. "Keep your pants on. I'll be right with you."

I went in through the front door, crossed a foyer floor that was waxed and polished to a mirror-like finish. I started up the stairs. They were polished to the same gleaming perfection as the floors, and I slipped perilously once when I stepped off of the carpet runner. For perhaps the thousandth time, I wondered how Ralph Devore found the time to maintain the house and grounds as he did. For he did do it all, everything that was done here and a hundred other things besides. Luane hadn't lifted a hand in years. It had been years since she had contributed a penny to maintaining the place.

There was a picture of them, Ralph and Luane, on the wall at the turn in the stairs. One of those enlarged, retouched photographs hung in an oval gilt frame. It had been taken twenty-two years before at the time of their marriage. In those days, Luane had resembled Theda Bara—if you remember your silent-motion-picture stars—and Ralph looked a lot like that Spanish lad, Ramon Navarro.

Ralph still looked pretty much as he had then but Luane did not. She was sixty-two now. He was forty.

Her bedroom extended across the front of the house, facing the town. Through its huge picture window, she could see just about everything that went on in Manduwoc. And judging by the gossip I'd heard (and she'd started), she not only saw everything that happened but a hell of a lot that didn't.

Her door was open. I went in and sat down, trying not to wrinkle my nose against that bedfast smell—the smell of stale sweat, stale food, rubbing alcohol, talcum and disinfectant. This was one room that Ralph could do nothing about. Luane hadn't left it since God knows when, and it was so cluttered you could hardly turn around in it.

There was a huge television set on one side of the room. On the other side was a massive radio, and next to it an elaborate hi-fi phonograph. They were operated from a remote control panel on a bedside table. Almost completely circling the bed were other tables and benches, loaded down variously with magazines, books, candy boxes, cigarettes, carafes, an electric toaster, coffee pot, chafing dish, and cartons and cans of food. Thus surrounded, with everything imaginable at her fingertips, Luane could make-do for herself during the long hours that Ralph was away. For that matter, she could have done so, anyhow. Because there was not a damned thing wrong with her. The local doctor said there wasn't. So did a diagnostician I'd once brought down from the city. The local man "treated" her, since she insisted on it. But there was nothing at all wrong with her. Nothing but self-pity and selfishness, viciousness and fear: the urge to lash out at others from the sanctuary of the invalid's bed.

I sat down near the window, and lighted a cigar. She sniffed distastefully, and I sniffed right back at her. "All right," I said. "Let's get it over with. What's the matter now?"

Her mouth worked. She took a grayish handkerchief from beneath her pillow, and blew into it. "It—it's R-Ralph, Kossy. He's planning to kill me!"

"Yeah?" I said. "So what's wrong with that?"

"He is, Kossy! I know you don't believe me, but he is!"

"Swell," I said. "You tell him if he needs any help just to give me a ring."

She looked at me helplessly, big fat tears filling her eyes. I grinned and gave her a wink.

"You see?" I said. "You talk stupid to me, and I'll talk stupid to you. And where the hell will that get us?"

"But it's not—I mean, it's true, Kossy! Why would I say so if it wasn't?"

"Because you want attention. Excitement. And you're too damned no-account to go after it like other people do." I hadn't meant to get rough with her. But she needed it—she had to be brought to her senses. And, I admit, I just couldn't help it. I very seldom lose my temper. I may act like it, but I very seldom do. But this time it was no act. "How the hell can you do it?" I said. "Ain't you done enough to the poor guy already? You marry him when he's eighteen. You talk his father, your caretaker, into geting him to marry you—"

"I did not! I—I—"

"The hell you didn't! The old man was ignorant; he thought he was doing the right thing by his son. Setting him up so that he could get a good education and amount to something. But how did it turn out? Why—"

"I gave Ralph a good home! Every advantage! It's not my fault that—"

"You didn't give him anything," I said. "Ralph worked for everything he got, and he helped support you besides. And he's still working anywhere from ten to twenty-four hours a day. Oh, sure, you've tossed the dough around. You've thrown away the whole damned estate. But Ralph never got any of it. It all went for Luane Devore, and to hell with Ralph."

She cried some more. Then she pouted. Then she pulled the injured dignity stunt. She *believed,* she said, that Ralph was *quite* satisfied with the way she had treated him. He'd married her because he loved her. He hadn't wanted to go away to school. He was never happier than when he was working. Under the circumstances, then . . .

Her voice trailed away, a look of foolish embarrassment spreading over her flabby, talcum-caked face. I nodded slowly.

"That just about wraps it up, doesn't it, Luane? You've said it all yourself."

"Well . . ." She hesitated. "Perhaps I do worry, brood too much. But—"

"Let's pin it down tight. Wrap it up once and for all. Just what reason would Ralph have to kill you? This place—all that's left of the estate? Huh-uh. He has it now, practically speaking. He'll have it legally when you die. After all the years he's slaved here, worked to improve it, you couldn't will it to someone else. You could, of course, but it wouldn't hold up in court. I— Yeah?"

"I—nothing." She hesitated again. "I'm pretty sure she couldn't be the reason. After all, he's only known her a couple of days."

"Who?" I said.

"A girl at the dance pavilion. The vocalist with the band this year. I'd heard that Ralph was driving her around a lot, but, of course—"

"So who doesn't he drive around when he gets a chance?" I said. "It's a way of picking up a few bucks."

She nodded that that was so. She agreed that most of Ralph's haul-and-carry customers were women, since women were less inclined to walk than men.

"Anyway," she added thoughtfully, "if it was just another woman—well, that couldn't be the reason, could it? He could just run away with her. He could get a divorce. He wouldn't have to—to—"

"Of course he wouldn't," I said. "And he doesn't want to, and he doesn't intend to. Where did you ever get the notion that he did, anyhow? Has he said anything, done anything, out of the way?"

She shook her head. She'd *thought* he'd been behaving rather oddly, and then she'd heard this gossip about the girl. And then she'd been feeling so poorly lately, sick to her stomach and unable to sleep nights, and—

The telephone rang. She broke off the recital of her various ailments, and snatched it up. She didn't talk long—not as long as she obviously wanted to. And what she did say was phrased obliquely. Still, with what I'd already heard in town, I was able to get the drift of the conversation.

She hung up the receiver. Keeping her eyes averted from mine, she thanked me for coming to see her. "I'm sorry to have bothered you, Kossy. I get so worried, you know, and then I get excited—"

"But you're all squared away now?" I said. "You know now that Ralph has no intention of killing you, that he never did have and never will have?"

"Yes, Kossy. And I can't tell you how much I—"

"Don't try," I said. "Don't tell me anything. Don't call me again. Because I'm not representing you any longer. You've gone too damned far this time."

"Why—why, Kossy." Her hand went to her mouth. "You're not angry with me j-just because . . ."

"I'm disgusted with you," I said. "You make me want to puke."

"But why? What did I do?" Her lower lip pulled down, piteously. "I lie here all day long, with nothing to do and no one to talk to . . . a sick, lonely old woman . . ."

She saw it wasn't going to work, that nothing she could say would square things between us. Her eyes glinted with sudden venom, and her whine shifted abruptly to a vicious snarl.

"All right, get out! Get out and stay out, and good riddance, you—*you hook-nosed little shyster!*"

"I'll give you a piece of advice first," I said. "You'd better stop telling those rotten lies about people before one of them stops you. Permanently, know what I mean?"

"Let them try!" she screamed. "I'd just like to see them try! I'll make things a lot hotter for 'em than they are now!"

I left. Her screeches and screams followed me down the stairs and out of the house.

I drove back to the cottage, and told Rosa the outcome of my visit. She listened to me, frowning.

"But, dear—do you think you should have done that? If she's that far gone, at the point where someone may kill her—"

"No one's going to, dammit," I said. "I was just trying to throw a scare into her. If anyone was going to kill her, they wouldn't have waited this long."

"But she's never gone this far before, has she?" Rosa shook her head. "I wish you hadn't done it. It—now, don't get angry—but it just isn't like you. She needs you, and when someone needs you . . ."

She smiled at me nervously. With a kind of nervous firmness. The cords in my throat began to tighten. I said what Luane Devore needed was a padded cell. She needed her tail kicked. She needed a psychiatrist, not a lawyer.

"What the hell?" I said. "Ain't I entitled to a vacation? I got to spend the whole goddamned summer with a poisoned-tongue maniac banging my ear? I don't get this," I said. "I thought you'd be pleased. First you raise hell because I'm going to see her, and now you raise hell because I'm not."

"So I talk a little," Rosa shrugged. "I'm a woman. That don't mean you should let me run your business."

I jumped up and danced around her. I puffed out my cheeks and rolled my eyes and fluttered my hands. "This is you," I said. "Mrs. Nutty Nonsense. You know so damned much, why ain't you a lawyer?"

"The great man," said Rosa. "Listen how the great attorney talks to his wife . . . I'm sorry, dear. You do whatever you think is right."

"And I'm sorry," I said. "I guess maybe I'm getting old. I guess things get on my nerves more than they used to. I guess—"

I guessed I might possibly have been a little hasty with Luane Devore.

"Don't let me influence you," Rosa said. "Don't do what you think I want you to. That way there is always trouble."

II

Ralph Devore

THE DAY I began thinking about killing Luane was the day the season opened. Which was also the day the dance pavilion opened, which was the day I met Danny Lee, who was the vocalist with Rags McGuire's orchestra. She was a she-vocalist even if her name was Danny. A lot of girl vocalists have boys' names. Take Janie, Rags' wife, who was always with the band until she had that bad accident—I mean, until this year, because there wasn't really any accident, Rags says. It was another party by the same name, and she is staying at home now to look after their boys who did not actually get killed after all. Well, Janie always sang under the name of Jan McGuire. I don't know why those girls do that, because everyone knows that they're girls—they do, anyway, as soon as they see them. And with Janie, you didn't even need to see her to know it. You could just feel it, I mean. You could just be in the same building with her, with your eyes closed maybe, and you'd know Janie was there. And, no, it wasn't because of her voice, because she had more kind of a man's voice than a woman's. What they call a contralto, or what they would call a contralto if she wasn't a pop singer. Because they don't seem to classify pop vocalists like they do the other kind. Rags was kidding when he said it—he used to kid around a lot—but he told me that Janie was the only girl singer in the country who wasn't a coloratura. Or, at least, a lyric soprano. He didn't know where the hell they all came from, he said, since there didn't used to be a coloratura come along more than once every ten years. Well, anyway, he can't say that any more; I mean, about Janie being the only girl who isn't a coloratura. Because Danny Lee isn't one either. She's got the same kind of voice that Janie had—only, well, kind of different—and she even kind of looks like Janie; only Rags gets sore when you say so, so I've never done it but once. Rags is awfully funny in some ways. Nice, you know, but funny. Now, me, when you like a person, when you think a lot of 'em, I think you ought to show it. I mean if you're me, you have to. You can't do anything else, and you wouldn't think of saying or doing anything to hurt them. But a lot of people are different, and Rags is one of them. Take with Janie. I know he thought the world of Janie, but he was all the time jumping on her. Always accusing her of something dirty. She couldn't look at anyone cross-eyed, just being pleasant, you know, without him saying she was running after the guy or something like that. And it just wasn't so. You wouldn't find a nicer girl than Janie in a month of Sundays. Oh, she drank a little, I guess. These last few years, she drank *quite* a bit. But—well, we'll leave that go a while.

Now, I was saying that I'd thought about killing Luane that first day of the season. But that isn't really the way it was. I mean, I didn't actually think about killing her. What I thought about was how it would be maybe if she wasn't there. I didn't want her not to be there exactly—to be dead —but still, well, you know. I started off wondering how it would be if she was, and then after a while I began kind of half-wishing that she was. And then, finally, I thought about different ways that she might be. Because if she wasn't— dead, I mean—I didn't know what I was going to do. And you put yourself in my place, and I don't think you'd have known either.

Usually—during the winter, anyway—I lay around in bed until five-thirty or six in the morning. But that day was the first of the season, so I was up at four. I dressed in the dark, and slipped out into the starlight. I did the chores, sort of humming and grinning to myself, feeling as tickled as a kid on Christmas morning. I felt good, I'll tell you. It was dark and the air was pretty nippy at that hour of the morning, but still everything seemed bright to me and I had that nice warm feeling inside. It was like I'd been buried in a cave, and I'd finally managed to get out. And that was kind of the way it was, too, in a way. Because this last winter had really been a bad one. Take the engineer's job at the courthouse, firing the boilers; now that's always been my job—an hour morning and evening and an hour on Saturday morning— but last winter it wasn't mine. And the school custodian job—four hours a day and two days once a month—that had always been mine, too, and now it wasn't. I talked to the head of the county commissioners, and he sent me to the county attorney. And the way he explained it—about the boilers—was that the commissioners could be held liable for any money they spent in excess of what was necessary. So automatic boilers were being installed, and that was that. I tried to argue with him, but it didn't do any good. It didn't do any good when I talked to the president of the school board, Doctor Ashton. They were dividing my job up among some of the vocational students. I wouldn't be needed now or at any time in the future, Doc said. And he gave me one of those straight, hard-eyed looks like the county attorney had.

So there I was. A hundred and fifty dollars a month gone down the drain. Practically every bit of my winter income, except for a little wood-cutting and stuff like that. Well, sure, I'd always kept a pretty big garden, canned and dried a lot of stuff. And, of course, there were the pigs, and we had our own eggs and milk and so on. And, naturally, I had some money put by. But, you know, you just can't figure that way; I mean, you can't count on standing on rock bottom. You do that, say, and what happens if things get worse? If a rainy day comes along, and that water that's only been up to your chin goes over your nose? Money can go mighty fast when you don't have any coming in. Say you run in the hole five dollars a day, why in a year's time that's almost two thousand dollars. And say you're forty like I am, and you've got maybe twenty-five years to live unless you starve to death . . . ! I tell you I was almost crazy with worry. Anyone would have been. But now it was the first day of the season, and all my worries were over—I thought. I'd just work a little harder, make enough to make up for what I didn't make during the winter, and everything would be fine. I mean, I thought it would be.

I finished my chores. Then I spread a big tarp in the back of the Mercedes-Benz, and put my mower and tools inside. You're probably wondering what a man like me is doing with a Mercedes, them being worth so much money. But the point is they're only worth a lot when you're buying; you go to sell one it's a different story. I did get a pretty good offer or two for it, back when I first got it—two seasons ago— but I kind of held on, thinking I might get a better one. And, of course, I liked it a lot, too, and I did need a car to get around in, to haul myself and my tools and passengers during the season. So, maybe it was the wrong thing, but it looked to me like I couldn't really lose since I'd gotten it for nothing. So, well, I've still got it.

The man who did own it was a writer, a motion-picture writer, who used to come up here for the season. He began having trouble with it right after I want to work for him, and he had me tinker on it for him; and it would run pretty good for a time and then it would go blooey again. He got pretty sore about it. I mean, he got sore at the car. One morning he got so mad he started to take an ax to it, and I guess he would have if I hadn't stopped him. Well, back then, there was a summer Rolls agency over at Atlantic Center—that's a pretty big place, probably ten times as big as Manduwoc. So I suggested to this writer that as long as he needed a car and he didn't like the Mercedes, why not let me tow him over there and see what kind of a trade-in he could get.

Well, you know how it is. Those dealers can stick just about any price tag on a car they want to. So this one said he could allow six thousand on the Mercedes (he just boosted the Rolls price that much), and the writer snapped him up on it. And as soon as he'd driven off, the dealer signed the Mercedes over to me. I tinkered with the motor a little. I've never had to touch it since.

Yes, this writer was pretty sore when he found out what had happened. He claimed I'd deliberately put the Mercedes on the blink, and he threatened to have both me and that dealer arrested. But he couldn't prove anything, so it didn't bother me that much. I mean, after all, a man that's got twenty-five or thirty thousand dollars to throw away on a car, has got blamed little to fuss about. And if he can't protect an investment like that, he shouldn't have it in the first place.

After I'd finished loading the Mercedes, I went in and did a quick job on the house. Which didn't take long since I'd slicked everything up good the night before. I ate breakfast, and then I fixed more breakfast and carried it up to Luane. We had a real nice talk while she ate. When she was through, I gave her a sponge bath, tickling her and teasing her until she was almost crying she laughed so hard. As a matter of fact, she did cry a little but not sad like she sometimes does. It was more kind of wondering, you know—like when you know something's true but you can't quite believe it.

"You like me, don't you?" she said. "You really do like me, don't you?"

"Well, sure," I said. "Of course. I don't need to tell you that."

"You've never regretted anything? Wished things had been different?"

"Regret what?" I said. "What would I want different?"

"Well—" She gestured. "To travel. See the world. Do something besides just work and eat and sleep."

"Why, I do a lot besides that," I said. "Anyway, what would I want to travel for when I've got everything I want right here?"

"Have you, darling?" She patted my cheek. "Do you have everything you want?"

I nodded. Maybe I didn't have everything I wanted right there in the house, her being pretty well along in years. But working like I do, I didn't have to hunt very hard to get it. Most of the time it was the other way around.

Well, anyway, I got her fixed up for the day with everything she might need, and then I left. Feeling good, like I said. Feeling like all my troubles were over. I drove up to Mr. J. B. Brockton's place, and started to work on the lawn. And in just about five minutes—just about the time it took him to get out of the house—all the good feeling was gone, and I knew I hadn't seen any trouble compared with what I was liable to.

"I'm sorry, Ralph," he said, sort of kicking at the grass with his toe. "I tried any number of times to reach you yesterday, but your phone was always tied up."

I shook my head. I just couldn't think of anything to say for a minute. He wasn't like some of the summer people I worked for—people who just order you around like you didn't have any feelings, and maybe make jokes about you —about the "natives"—in front of their company. He was more like a friend, you know. I liked him, and he went out of his way to show that he liked me. Why, just last season he'd given me a couple suits. Two hundred and fifty dollar suits, he said they were. And, of course, he was probably exaggerating a little. Because how could just a suit of clothes cost two hundred and fifty? But even if they only cost fifty or seventy-five, it was a mighty handsome gift. Not something you'd give to people unless you thought an awful lot of them.

"Mr. Brockton," I said. And that was as far as I could go for a minute. "Mr. Brockton, what's the matter?"

"Well, I'll tell you, Ralph," he said, not looking at me, still kicking at the grass. "Doctor Ashton's son got in touch with me by mail a week or so ago. I've decided to give the work to him."

Well. You could have pushed me over with a dew drop. I didn't know whether to laugh or cry.

"Bobbie Ashton?" I said. "Why—what would Bobbie be doing doing yard work? Why, he must have been joking you, Mr. Brockton! Doc Ashton, why, he always hires his own yard work done, so why would Bobbie—"

"I've already engaged him," Mr. Brockton said. "It's all settled. I'm sorry, Ralph." He hesitated a second; then he said, "I think Doctor Ashton is a good man. I think Bob is a fine boy."

"Well, so do I," I said. "You never heard me say anything else, Mr. Brockton."

"I like them," he said. "And I came here to rest, to enjoy myself. And I do not like—in fact, I refuse, Ralph—to be drawn into community quarrels."

I knew what the trouble was then. I knew there was nothing I could do about it. All I could do now was to get to some other place as fast as I could. So . . . so I made myself smile. I said I could see how he might feel, and that he shouldn't feel bad about it on my account. Then I started reloading the Mercedes.

"Ralph," he said. "Wait a minute."

"Yes, sir?" I turned back around.

"I can give you a job with my company. In one of our factories. Something that you could do, and that would pay quite well."

"Oh?" I said. "You mean in New York City, Mr. Brockton?"

"Or New Jersey. Newark. I think you'd like it, Ralph. I think it would be the best thing that ever happened to you."

"Yes, sir," I said. "I guess you're probably right, Mr. Brockton, and I sure do appreciate the offer. But I guess not."

"You guess not?" he said. "Why not?"

"Well, I—I just guess I hadn't better," I said. "You see, I never lived anywhere but here. I've never been any further away than Atlantic Center, and that was just for a couple of hours. And just being away that far, that little time, I was so rattled and mixed up it was two-three days before I could calm down."

"Oh, well," he shrugged. "You'd get over that."

"I guess not," I said. "I mean, I *can't*, Mr. Brockton. It's kind of like I was rooted here, like I was one of them—those—shrubs. You try to put me down somewhere else, and—"

"Oh, I'm not trying to! Far be it from me to persuade a man against his will."

He nodded, kind of huffy-like, and headed for the house. I drove away. I knew he was probably right. I kind of wished I could leave Manduwoc—just kind of, you know. And before that day was much older I was really wishing it, with hardly any kind-of at all. But there just wasn't any way that I could.

Luane would never leave here. Even if she would, what good would it do? Any place we went, people would laugh and talk about us like they'd always done here. There'd be the same stories. Well, not exactly the same, I guess, because outsiders wouldn't know about Pa. So they wouldn't be apt to say that Pa and Luane, well—that I was really her son instead of her husband. Or, her son as well as her husband. But however it was, it would be bad. And Luane would start striking back twice as hard, like she'd struck back here. Probably she'd do it anyhow, even if people did have the good manners and kindness to keep their mouths shut. Because she'd been the way she was now for so long, she'd lost the knack for being any other way.

I felt awful sorry for Luane. She'd sure given up a lot on my account. She was a lady, and she came from a proud old family. She'd been a good church-goer and a charity-worker, and everything like that. And then just because she wanted someone to love before she got too old for it, why there was all that dirtiness. Stuff that took the starch right out of you, and filled you up with something else. No, it didn't bother me too much; I guess I just didn't have enough sense to be bothered, and, of course, I never amounted to anything to begin with. But it did something pretty terrible to Luane. She didn't show it for a long time, except maybe a little around me. She had too much pride. But the hurt was there inside, festering and spreading, and finally breaking out. And then really getting bad. Getting a little worse the older she got.

I sure wished Luane could go away with me. I figured I could make out pretty fine with Luane. With someone like that, you know, someone who knew her way around and could tell you what to do—someone that really loved you and you could talk to, and—and . . .

Well, I guess I just hadn't wanted to face the facts there at Mr. J. B. Brockton's place. I mean, it was such an awful setback, I didn't feel like I could bear any more; I just couldn't admit that it would be the same way wherever else I went. Because what was I going to do if it was? How was I going to live? What would I do if I couldn't make out here, and I couldn't go any place else?

You can see how I'd be kind of stunned. So scared that I couldn't look at the truth even with my nose rubbed in it.

So, anyway, I went on to all the other estates. I made them all, just taking "no" for an answer at first, and then arguing and finally begging. And, of course, it was the same story everywhere. I was just wasting my breath and my time. They were sorry, sure; most of 'em said they were, anyhow. But Bobbie Ashton had asked for the work, and Doc Ashton was an influential man—and he treated most of them—so Bobbie was going to get it.

It was noon by the time I'd gone to the last place I could go to. I drove down to the beach and ate the lunch I'd packed that morning. Gulping it down, not really tasting it.

Twenty-five years, I thought. Twenty-five years, but no, a man like me would probably live a lot longer than that. Thirty-five or forty, probably. Maybe even fifty or sixty. Fifty or sixty years with everything going out and nothing coming in!

Yes, there was a little work around town, for the local

residents, you know. But it wasn't worth bothering with. Just fifty cents here and a dollar there. Anyway, the kids had it all sewed up.

I wondered if it would do any good for me to talk to Bobbie, but I didn't wonder long. He'd made up his mind to run me out of town—to get back at Luane through me.

Doc Ashton settled here a little short of seventeen years ago. His wife had died in childbirth, so he had this Negro wet nurse for Bobbie, the woman who still works for them as housekeeper. Doc was quite a young man then. The woman was young, too—in fact, she's still fairly young— and pretty good-looking, besides.

Well, Bobbie was sick when he got here, the colic or something. And he no sooner got over that than he was hit by something else. Every disease you ever heard of practically, why Bobbie had it. One right after another. Year after year. He couldn't play with other kids, couldn't go to school; he was hardly out of the house for almost twelve years. Then, finally, I guess because he'd had every blamed sickness there was to get, he didn't get any more. He began to shoot up and broaden out. All at once, he was just about the healthiest, huskiest—and handsomest—kid you ever saw in your life. And smart! You couldn't believe a kid could be that smart, and probably you won't find many that are.

I suppose he got a lot of it from all those books he'd read when he couldn't do anything else. But there was plenty more to Bobbie's smartness than book-learning. He just seemed to have been born with a head on him, a head with all the answers. He could do things before being told how or reading about 'em, or maybe even hearing of 'em before. Not just lessons, you know, but *anything!*

He went through eight grades of grammar school in a year. He went through high school in a year and a half. At least he could have gone through, if he hadn't dropped out the last semester. Now, it didn't look like he'd be going to college; he wouldn't be studying to be a doctor. And how Doc Ashton would be feeling about that, I hated to think.

* * *

I wadded up my lunch sack, and put it in a trash basket. Then, I got a drink of water from one of the picnicker fountains, and drove up to the dance pavilion.

The big front doors were swung open. I went inside, circled around in front of the bandstand, and stopped in the doorway of Pete Pavlov's office. He was at his desk, bent over some papers. He glanced up, squirted a stream of tobacco into a spittoon and bent back over the papers again.

He's one of those round-faced, square-built men. About fifty, I guess. He wore khaki pants with both a belt and suspenders, and a blue work shirt with a black bow tie. His hair was parted on the side, and there was a blob of shaving soap up around one of the temples.

I waited. I began to get a little uneasy, even though I was practically sure that I had a job with him for the summer. Because any time Pete Pavlov could do anything to annoy people in Manduwoc, he was just about certain to do it. I mean, he'd go out of his way to get under their hides. And giving me work would get under 'em bad.

He didn't need to care what they thought of him; his business was all with the summer trade. He owned most of the rent cottages, and the pavilion, and two of the hotels, and oh, probably, two-thirds of the concession buildings. So to heck with Manduwoc, was the way he felt. The town people hadn't ever done anything for him. In fact, they'd always been kind of down on him, sort of resentful. Because even back when he was a day laborer, cleaning out cesspools or anything he could get to do, he was independent as a hog on ice. He'd do a good day's work, but he wouldn't say thankyou for his pay. If anyone called him by his first name or just Pavlov, he'd do exactly the same thing with them. No matter who they were or how much money they had.

He straightened up from his desk, and looked at me. I smiled and said hello, and remarked that it was a nice day. I said, "I guess I better be getting to work, hadn't I, Pete?"

He waited for me to say something else. I didn't, because I was just too worried. Here was maybe another twenty-five dollars a week going down the hole. The only chance I had left for any income.

Pete kind of squirmed around in his chair, kind of scratching his rear, I guess. He leaned back and picked something out of his nose, and held it up and looked at it. And then he pushed his lips out, moved them in and out, while he stared down at his desk.

"Well, hell," he said. "I tell you how it is, Ralph. The way this goddamned summer business is going, I figure on hiring out myself."

I didn't say anything. I guessed things weren't as good for him as they used to be, but I knew he was still setting pretty. He had plenty, all right, Pete Pavlov did. It would take more than a few slack seasons to hurt him much.

"What are you looking like that for?" he said. "You think I'm a goddamned liar?" Then, his eye flickered and shifted, and he let out a whoop of laughter, and slapped his hand down on his desk. "Well, you're right, by God! I wish you could have seen your face! Really had you going, didn't I?"

"Aw, no, you didn't," I said. "I knew you were joking all the time."

"You know what a broom looks like?" He waved me toward the door. "Well, see if you can find one that'll fit your hands."

I got out. I got busy on the restrooms, and after a while, as he was leaving for downtown, he looked in on me. Stood around talking and joking for a few minutes. He asked about Luane, and said he was pretty goddamned hurt the way she never told any dirty stories about him. I laughed, kind of uncomfortable, and said I guessed that was his fault, not hers. Which was mainly the way it was, of course. Because how can you mud a man up when he's already covered himself with it? To annoy people, you know. What's the point in saying that a man does such and such or so and so when he lets 'em all know it himself?

He had a family, a wife and daughter, but Luane couldn't do much to dirty them, either. There just wasn't enough to them, you know, to hold dirt. They were dowdy and drab.

They went around with their shoulders slumped and their heads bowed—like they might cut and run if you looked their way. No one was interested in them. There wasn't anything to be interested in. And if the time ever came when there was, well, I figured Luane would do some tall thinking before she gossiped about it.

You see, years ago—before Luane and I were married—her father gave Pete an awful raw deal. Cheated him out of a pile of money, and then placed it in Luane's name, so that Pete couldn't sue. Luane's always felt kind of guilty about it. She'd think a long time before she did anything else to hurt Pete or his family.

"Well," Pete said. "I got a feeling that this may be a good season after all. The best damned season yet."

"I think it will, too," I said. "I think you're right, Pete."

He left. I finished with the washrooms, and went back to his office.

I pulled a chair up to the air-vent, took off the grate and crawled up inside the duct. I crawled through it slowly, squirming along on my stomach, brushing all the dust and cobwebs and dead bugs in front of me. It was so hot and stuffy I could hardly breathe, and I kept sneezing and bumping my head; and I was just about one big muddy smear of sweat and dust. I crawled through all the duct, the branches and the main, and came out at the rear of the building.

I dropped down to the roof of the blower shed. I started up the big four-horse motor, tightened the belt to the fan, and went in the back door of the men's room.

I looked at myself in the mirror, and, man, was I a mess! Dirt and cobwebs from head to foot. I started to turn on the water at one of the sinks, and then I stopped with my hand a couple of inches away—kind of frozen in the air. I stood that way for a few seconds, listening to the piano, to Rags, listening to *her*. Then I turned toward the door, picking up my broom sort of automatically, and went out into the ballroom.

It was pretty shadowed in there, and there was just the swivel-necked light on over the piano. So, for a second, I thought it was Janie up there singing. Then I started across the floor, and pretty soon I saw it was another girl. She had the same kind of voice as Janie, and the same kind of candy-colored hair. But she was quite a bit bigger. I don't mean she was any taller or that she probably weighed any more, but still she was bigger. In certain places, you know. You could see that she was without even half-way studying the matter. Because it was still pretty warm there in the ballroom, and Rags was stripped to the waist. And all she had on was a bra and a little skimpy pair of shorts.

I thought she was a mighty good singer, but I knew Rags wasn't pleased with her. I knew because he was putting her through *Stardust*, having her rehearse it when he'd always told me that no singer needed to. "That's one they can't bitch up, see?" he'd told me. "They can do it with all the others. But *Stardust*, huh-uh."

He brought his hands down on the keys suddenly. With just a big crash. She stopped singing and turned toward him, her face hard and sullen-looking.

"All right," Rags said. "You win, baby. I'll send for Liberace. Me, I'm too old to run races."

"I'm sorry," she mumbled, not looking a darned bit sorry.

"Never mind that sorry stuff," he said. "Your name's Lee, ain't it? Danny Lee, ain't it?"

"You know what it is," she said.

"I'm asking you," he said. "It's not Carmichael or Porter or Mercer, is it? This ain't your music, is it? You've got no right to bitch it up, have you? You're goddamned right, you haven't! It's theirs—they made it, and the way they made it is the way it should be. So cut out the embroidery. Cut out that bar-ahead stuff. Just get with it, and stay with it!"

He picked up his cigarette from the piano, and tucked it into the corner of his mouth. He brought his hands down on the keys. He seemed to kind of stroke them—the keys, I mean. But yet there was no running together. Every note came through, clear and firm, soft but sharp. So smooth and easy and sweet.

Danny Lee took a deep breath. She held it, the bra

swelled full and tight. She was nodding her head with the music, tapping one toe. Listening, and then opening her mouth and letting her breath out in the *Stardust* words. Soft-husky. Pushing them out from down deep inside. Letting them float out with that husky softness, still warm and sweet from the place they'd been.

I looked at Rags. His eyes were closed, and there was a smile on his lips. I looked back at the girl, and I kind of frowned.

She didn't hardly have to move at all, to look like she was moving a lot. And she was moving a lot now. And if there was one thing that burned Rags McGuire up, it was that. He said it was cheap. He said singers who did that were acrobats.

Rags opened his eyes. His smile went away, and he lifted his hands from the keys and laid them in his lap. He didn't curse. He didn't yell. For a minute he hardly seemed to move, and the silence was so thick you could cut it with a knife. Then he motioned for her to come over to the piano. She hesitated, then went over, kind of dragging her feet, sullen and hard-faced, and watchful-looking.

And then Rags reamed her out—real hard. It was pretty rough.

She took her place again. Rags brought his hands down on the keys, and she began to sing. I moved in close. Rags gave me a little nod. I stood up close, drinking her voice in, drinking her in.

She finished the song. Without thinking how it might seem to Rags—like I might be butting in, you know—I busted out clapping. It had been so nice, I just had to.

Rags' eyes narrowed. Then he grinned and made a gesture toward me. "Okay, baby, take off," he said. "You've passed the acid test."

I guess he meant it as kind of an insult. Just to her, of course, because he and I are good friends, and always kidding around a lot. Anyway, she started down at me—and gosh, I'd forgot all about what a mess I was. And then she whirled around, bent over and stuck out her bottom at me. Kind of wiggled at me.

Rags let out a whoop. He whooped with laughter, banging his fists down on the top of the piano. Making so much noise that you couldn't hear what she was yelling, although I guess it was mostly cuss words.

He was still whooping and pounding as she marched back across the bandstand, and down the steps to the dressing room.

I grinned, or tried to. Feeling a little funny naturally, but not at all mad.

III

Rags McGuire

I SAW HER for the first time about four months ago. It was in a place in Fort Worth, far out on West Seventh Street. I wasn't looking for her or it, or anything. I'd just started walking that night, and when I'd walked as far as I could I was in front of this place. So I went inside.

There was a small bar up front. In the rear was a latticed-off, open roof area, with a lot of tables and a crowd of beer drinkers. I sat down and ordered a stein.

The waitress came with it. Another woman came right behind her, and helped herself to a chair. She was a pretty wretched-looking bag; not that it would have meant anything to me if she hadn't been. I gave her a couple bucks, and said no, thanks. She went away, and the three-piece group on the bandstand—sax, piano and drums—went back to work.

They weren't good, of course, but they were Dixieland. They played the music, and that's something. They played the music—or tried to—and these days that's really something.

They did *Sugar Blues* and *Wang Wang*, and *Goofus*. There

was a kitty on the bandstand, a replica of a cat's hat with a
PLEASE FEED THE sign. So, at intermission, I sent the
waitress up with a twenty-dollar bill.

I didn't notice that it was a twenty until it was in her hand.
I'd meant to make it a five—which was a hell of a lot more
than I could afford. Anything was a lot more than I could
afford. But she already had it, and you don't hear the music
much any more. So I let it go.

The waitress pointed me out to them. They all stood up
and smiled and bowed to me, and for a moment I was stupid
enough to think that they knew who I was. For, naturally,
they didn't. They don't know you any more if you play the
music. Only the players of crap, the atonal clashbang off-
key stuff that Saint Vitus himself couldn't dance to. To these
lads I was just a big spender. That's all I was to anyone in
the place.

I saw the waitress go over to a table in the corner. There
was a man seated at it, facing me, a guy with a beer-bleared
face and a suit that must have cost all of eighteen dollars.
There was also a girl, her back turned my way. The waitress
whispered to her, and the girl got up. Her companion made
noises of protest, and a burly, shirt-sleeved character, who
had been lurking in the vicinity, grabbed him by the collar
and hustled him out.

The girl started toward the bandstand. There was a small
burst of hand-clapping and stein-thumping. And my eyes
snapped open and my heart pounded, and I half rose out of
my chair. And then I settled back down again. Because, of
course, it wasn't Janie. Janie wouldn't be in a joint like this,
she wouldn't be hanging around with bar-flies. Anyway, I
knew where Janie was, at home looking after the boys,
whoring and guzzling and . . .

Janie was back in New York. I'd talked to her long-distance that night—had her sing to me over the telephone. It
was *Melancholy Baby,* one of our all-time hit recordings,
one of the dozen-odd which still sell considerably—and
thank God they do. Although I don't know who the hell
buys them. Probably they all go to insane asylums, the pa-

tients there. It must be that way, the poor devils must all be locked up, since there seems to be nothing on the outside any more but tone-deaf morons.

Why, goddammit, I talked to a man a while back, one of those pseudo-erudite bastards who is mopping up with articles about modern "music," the so-called up-beat, "cool" crap. I said, let me ask you something. Suppose the printer started "interpreting" your articles. Suppose he started leaving out lines and putting in his own, suppose he threw away your punctuation and put in his own. How would you feel if he did that, an "interpretation" of your stuff?

I shouldn't have wasted my time on him, of course. I shouldn't even have spit on him. He called himself a music critic—a critic, by God!—and he'd never heard of Blue Steele!

The girl didn't look like Janie. Not the slightest. I'd only thought she did at the time.

She sang. It was *Don't Get Around Much Any More,* another old hit of Janie's and mine. And she bitched it up. Brother, did she bitch it! But when I closed my eyes . . .

She had a voice. She had what it took, raw and undeveloped as it was. And she hit you. That's the only way I can say it—she hit you. She brought out the goosebumps, like that first blast of air when you step into an air-conditioned room.

And God knows I don't expect much. I work for something good, I do my best to get it. But I don't really expect it.

I began to get a little excited. I did some fast mental calculations. I was working single at the moment, doing a series of club dates. And I was just squeaking by. But the resort season wasn't too far off, and I had some recording checks due; and it would be easy enough to whip together another band. I could just about swing it, I thought. A five man combo, including myself, and this girl. I couldn't make any money with it, not playing the music. I'd be very lucky, in fact, if I could break even. But I *could* do it—do something, by God, that needed to be done. Give this mixed-up world something that it ought to have, regardless of whether it knew it or wanted it.

She finished the song. She was at my table before I could motion to her. I was still wrapped up in my calculations. I heard her pitch, but it was a minute or two before it sank in on me. And perhaps I should have expected it; and perhaps, by God, I should not have. From some girls, yes. From any other girl. But not her, not someone with the music in them.

I wanted to spit on her. I wanted to break my stein, slash her throat with it so that she would never sing another word. Instead, I said, fine: I hated sleeping by myself.

I suppose my expression had startled her. At any rate, she drew back a little. She didn't mean *that,* she said. All she meant was that maybe I could buy her dinner some place and we could have a nice visit, since she was alone, too, and maybe I could help her buy a new dress because a drunk had spilt some beer on this one, and—

She was really a nice girl. She told me so herself. She was just doing this (temporarily, of course!) because her mother was awfully sick— a sick mother, no less!—and she had a couple of younger brothers to support, and her father was dead and crops had been awfully bad on this farm she came from. And so on, ad infinitum, ad nauseam. The only thing she spared me was the fine-old-Southern-family routine. If she'd pulled that I think I *would* have killed her.

I took a couple of twenties out of my wallet and riffled them.

She simpered around a little more, and then she went back to my hotel with me.

I looked at her, and suddenly I turned and ducked into the bathroom. I hunched over, hugging my stomach, feeling my guts twist and knot themselves, wanting to scream with the pain. I puked, and wept silently. And it was better, then. I washed my face, and went back into the bedroom.

I told her to get her clothes on. I told her what I could and would do for her.

All the clothes she'd need; good clothes. A year's contract at two hundred dollars a week. Yes, two hundred dollars a week. And a chance to make something of herself, a chance eventually to make two thousand, five thousand, ten thousand. More than a chance, an absolute certainty. Because I *would* make something of her; I would not let her fail.

She believed me. People usually do believe me if I care to make the effort. Still, she hung back, apparently too shocked by the break I was offering her to immediately accept it. I gave her twenty dollars, promised her another twenty to meet me at the club in the morning. She did so—we had the place to ourselves except for the cleaning people—and I gave her a sample of what I could do for her.

A good sample, because I wanted her firmly hooked. With what I had in mind, the two hundred a week might not be enough to hold her. That invalid mother and two brothers et cetera, not withstanding. I wanted to give her a glimpse of the mint, boost her high enough up the wall so that even a whoring moron such as she could see it.

And I did.

I worked with her a couple hours. At the end of that time, she was no longer terrible, but merely bad. Which to her, of course, seemed nothing less than wonderful.

She was beaming and bubbling, and the sun seemed to have risen behind her eyes.

"I can hardly believe it!" she said. "It seems kind of like magic—like a beautiful dream!"

"The dream will get better," I said. "It will come true. Assuming, that is, that you want to accept my offer."

"Oh, I do! You know I do," she said. "I don't know how to thank you, Mr. McGuire."

I told her not to bother; she didn't owe me any thanks. We went back to my room, and I closed and locked the door.

She seemed to crumple a little, grow smaller, and the sun went out of her eyes. She stammered, that she wouldn't do it, then that she didn't want to. Finally, as I waited, she asked if she had to.

"I've never done anything like that before. Honestly, I haven't, Mr. McGuire! Only once, anyway, and it wasn't for money. I was in love with him, this boy back in my home town, and we were supposed to be married. And then he went away, and I thought I was pregnant so I left, and—"

"Never mind," I said. "If you don't want to . . ."

"And it'll be all right?" She looked at me anxiously. "You'll still—s-still—?"

I didn't say anything.

"W-will it? Will it, Mr. McGuire? Please, please! If you only knew . . ."

If I only knew, believed, that she was really a good girl. If I only knew how much she wanted to sing, how much this meant to her. You know.

I shrugged, remained silent. But inside I was praying. And what I was praying was that she would tell me to go to hell. I could have got down and kissed her feet for that, if she had insisted on being what the good Lord had meant her to be or being nothing; keeping the music undefiled or keeping it silent where it was. If only it had meant that much to her, as much as it meant to me—

And it didn't. It never means as much, even a fraction as much, as it means to me. Not to Janie. Not to anyone.

No one cares about the music.

Except for me it would vanish, and there would be no more.

Slowly, she unbuttoned her dress. Slowly, she pulled it down off one shoulder. I stared at her, grinning—wanting to yell and wanting to weep. And blackness swam up on me from the floor, dropped down over me from above.

I came out of it.

She was kneeling in front of me. My head was against her, and she was wet with my tears. And she was crying, and holding me.

"Mister McGuire . . . W-what's the matter, M-Mist— Oh, darling, baby, honey-lamb! What can I—"

She brushed her lips against my forehead, stroked my hair, whispering:

"Better now, sweetheart? Is Danny's dearest honey-pie bet—"

"You rotten, low-down little whore," I said.

* * *

Pete Pavlov was waiting at the station when we came in late Thursday night. The boys and Danny went on down to their cottages, and I went to his office with him.

I like Pete. I like his bluntness, his going straight to the point of a matter. There is no compromise about him. He knows what he wants and he will take nothing else, and whether it suits anyone else makes not the damnedest bit of difference to him.

He did not ask about Janie, nor the why of the new band. That was my business, and Pete minds his own business. He simply poured us a couple whopping drinks, tossed me a cigar and asked me if I knew where he could lay his hands on a fast ten or twenty thousand.

I said I wished I did. He shrugged and said he didn't really suppose I would, and just to forget he'd said anything. Then he said, "Excuse me, Mac"—Pete has always called me Mac—"Know I didn't need to tell *you* to keep quiet."

"That's okay," I said. "Things pretty bad, Pete?"

He said they were goddamned bad. So bad that he'd fire his hotels if he could collect on them. "Those goddamned insurance companies," he said. "Y'know, I figure that's why so many people get burned to death. Because the companies won't pay off on empty buildings. Guess I should have fired mine while they were open, but I kind of hated to take a chance on roasting someone."

I laughed, and shook my head. I hardly knew what to say. I knew what I should say, but I wasn't quite up to saying it, hard-pressed as I was.

He went on to explain his situation. He'd never borrowed any money locally. He'd always done business on a cash basis. Then, when things began to tighten up, he'd gone to some New York factors; and now the interest was murdering him.

"No usury laws when it comes to business loans, y'know. Did you know that? Well, that's the way she stands. I don't get up ten, twenty thousand, I'm just about going to be wiped out." He took a chew of tobacco, grunted sardonically. "Own damned fault, I guess. Too goddamned stubborn. Should have unloaded when things first started slipping."

"You couldn't have done it, Pete," I said. "If you knew how to give up, you'd never have got to where you are."

He said he guessed that was so. Guessed he didn't know how to lay down, and didn't want to learn.

"Pete," I said. "Look. Your contract is with the agency, and I can't cut the price. But I can rebate on it."

"Hell with you," he said. "You ugly, ornery, over-grown bastard."

He walked around the room, grunting that there were too damned many throats in need of cutting, without bleeding some dull-witted son-of-a-bitch like me who ought to have a guardian looking after him.

"Nope," he said, turning back around. "I ain't that bad off. If I was, I just wouldn't have signed up for you this year."

"Maybe you shouldn't have," I said. "And look, Pete. You can't break that contract, but if I should refuse to play—"

"Nope. No, now listen to me," he said. "I wouldn't do it, even if I didn't like to listen to that damned pounding of yours. I got to keep the pavilion open. Once I closed it, it'd be kind of a signal. I might as well paint a bullseye on my butt, and tell 'em all to start kicking."

We went on drinking and talking. Talking of things in general, and nothing much in particular. He said that when Kossmeyer came down the three of us ought to get together some night and have us a bull session. I said I'd like that—some time when I was feeling good and didn't have anything on my mind.

"I like him," I said. "He's a hell of an interesting little guy, and a nice one. But sometimes, y'know, Pete, I get a feeling that he ain't where I'm seeing him. I mean, he's right in front of me, but it seems like he's walking all around me. Looking me over. Staring through the back of my head."

Pete laughed. "He gives you that feeling too, huh? Ain't it funny, Mac? All the people there are in the world, and how many there are you can just sit down and cut loose and be yourself with."

I said it certainly was funny. Or tragic.

"Well, hell," he said, finally, "and three is seven. Daddy's gone and went to heaven. Guess you and me ought to be getting some sleep, Mac."

We said good-night, and he went off toward town, his chunky body moving in a straight line. I went to my cottage, feeling conscience-stricken and depressed by my failure to help him. By my failures period. Bitch and botch, that was me. In common honesty I ought to start billing myself that way: Bitch And Botch And His Band And Bitch. I could work up a theme song out of it, set it to the melody of—well, *Goodie Goodie*. Let's see, now, Tatuh ta ta tum, tatuh . . . I worked on that for a minute, and then swore softly to myself. I couldn't do anything right any more. Not the simplest, damnedest ordinary thing.

Take tonight, for example. My people were new here; there are rows and rows of cottages, all exactly alike. Yet I hadn't bothered to see that they got to the right ones, to see that they were comfortably settled. I'd just gone my own merry way—thinking only of myself—and to hell with them.

It didn't matter, of course, about Danny Lee. She could sleep on the beach for all I cared. But my men, poor bastards, were a different matter. They had enough to bear as it was—those sad, sad bastards. Just barely squeaking by, year after year. Working for the minimum, and tickled to death to get it. Big-talking and bragging, when they know —for certainly they must know—that they were unfitted to wipe a real musician's tail.

It must be very hard to maintain a masquerade like that. I felt very sorry for them, my men, and I was very gentle with them. They had no talent, nothing to build on, nothing to give. There can be nothing more terrible, it seems to me, than having nothing to give.

I unpacked my suitcases, and climbed into bed.

I fell asleep, slipping almost immediately into that old

familiar dream where everyone in the band was me. I was on
the trumpet, the sax-and-clarinet. I was on the trombone,
at the drums, and, of course, the piano. All of us were me
—the whole combo. And Danny Lee-Janie was the vocalist,
but she-they were also me. And it was not perfect, the music
was not quite perfect. But it was close, so close, by God!
All we-I needed was a little more time—time is all it takes
if you have it to work with—and . . .

I woke up.

It was a little after twelve, noon. The smell of coffee
drifted through my window, along with snatches of conversation.

It came from the boys' cabin—they were batching together to save money. They were keeping their voices low,
and our cottages, like the others, were thirty feet apart.
("Don't like to be crowded," Pete told me, "and don't figure
anyone else does.") But sound carries farther around water:

*"Did you hear what he said to me, claimin' I had a lip?
Why, goddammit, I been playin' trumpet . . ."*

*"Hell, you got off easy! What about him asking me if
I had rheumatism, and I needed a hammer to close the
valves . . .?"*

*"The wild-eyed bastard is crazy that's all! I leave it to
you, Charlie. You ever hear me slide in or off a note? I ever
have to feel for 'em? Why . . ."*

They were all chiming in, trying to top one another. But
the drummer finally got and held the floor. I listened to his
complaints—the bitter low-pitched voice. And I was both
startled and hurt.

Possibly I had seemed a little sharp to the others, but I
certainly hadn't meant to. I had only been joking, trying to
make light of something that could not be helped. With the
drummer, however, I had been especially gentle—exceed-
ingly careful to do or say nothing that might hurt his pride.
He had nothing at all to feel bitter about that I could see.

It was true that I had joked with him, but in the mildest of
ways. I had not so much corrected him as tried to get him to
correct himself.

I had tossed him a bag of peanuts on one occasion. On a couple of others I had suddenly held a mirror in front of him, at the height of his idiotic, orgiastic contortions. I had had him look at himself, that was all. I had said nothing. It was pointless to say anything, since English was even more than a mystery to him than music, and I saw no necessity to. It seemed best simply to let him look at himself—at the man become monkey. And how that could possibly have made him sore, why he should blame me for the way he looked . . .

Well, the hell with it. He wasn't worth worrying about or bothering with. None of them were. Only Danny Lee— Danny Lee's voice. I wished to God I could have gotten hold of her a couple of years sooner. By now, she'd have been at the top, so good that she wouldn't have been caught dead in a place like this.

I shaved and bathed and dressed. I walked over to her cottage, and told her to show at the pavilion at two o'clock sharp.

Then I dropped in on the boys.

They saw or heard me coming, for their voices rose suddenly in awkward self-conscious conversation. I went in, and there was a stilted exchange of greetings, and a heavy silence. And then two of them offered me coffee at the same time.

I declined, said I was eating in town. "By the way," I added. "Can I do anything for you guys in town? Mail some letters to the local for you?"

They knew I'd heard them then. I looked at them smiling, one eyebrow cocked; glancing from one sheepish, reddening, silly face to another.

No one said a word. No one made a move. They almost seemed to have stopped breathing. And I stared at them, and suddenly I was sick with shame.

I mumbled that everything was Jake. I told them they'd better get out and have some fun; to rent a boat, buy some swim trunks—anything they needed—and to charge it to me.

"No rehearsal today," I said. "None any day."

I got out of there.

I ate and went to the pavilion, and went to work with Danny Lee.

After a while, Ralph Devore showed up.

Ralph's the handyman-janitor here. Also the floorman— the guy who moves around among the dancers, and maintains order and so on. He's a hell of a handsome guy, vaguely reminiscent of someone I seem to have seen in pictures. He has a convertible Mercedes, which, I understand, he got through some elaborate chiseling. And dressed up in those fancy duds he has (give to him by wealthy summer people) he looks like a matinee idol. But he wasn't dressed up now. Now, when Danny Lee was seeing him for the first time, he looked like Bowery Bill from Trashcan Hill.

She was so burned up when he gave her a hand—and I kidded her about it—that she flounced her butt at him.

She stomped off to the dressing room. Ralph and I chewed the fat a little. And I began to get a very sweet idea, a plan for giving Miss Danny her comeuppance. I could see that Ralph had fallen for her. He wanted her so bad he could taste it. So with him looking as he did—or could—and Danny being what she was . . .

I put it up to Ralph, giving him slightly less than the facts about Danny. I said that she not only looked like a nice girl, but she *was* one. Very nice. The sole support of her family, in fact. So how did that cut any ice? He wasn't going to rape her. He could just take her out, and leave the rest up to her. If she wanted to cut loose okay, and if not the same.

"Well . . ." He hesitated nervously. "It just don't somehow seem right, Rags; I mean, fooling a nice little girl like that. I don't like people foolin' me, and—"

"So where's the harm?" I said. "If she really wants to hang on to it, money won't make any difference to her. If it does make a difference—all the dough you're supposed to have—there's still no harm done. What she loses can't be worth much."

"Well, yeah," he said. "Yeah, but . . ."

I was afraid he was going to ask why my enthusiasm for the enterprise. But I needn't have worried. He was too absorbed in Danny, so hard hit that he was in kind of a trance. And vaguely, with part of my mind, I wondered about that.

Ralph had seen sexy babes before. Seen them and had them. They were invariably kitchen maids or shop-girls on an outing, but still they had what it took. All that Ralph, being married, was interested in.

"She looks kind of tough," he murmured absently. "Awful sweet, kind of, but tough. Like she could be plenty hard-boiled if she took the notion."

"Oh, well," I said. "Think what a hard time she's had. Supporting an invalid mother and—"

"I bet she knows her way around, don't she?"

"And you'd win," I said. "She can take care of herself, Ralph. You won't be taking advantage of her at all."

"Well . . ." He squirmed indecisively. "I—I— What you want me to do?"

He had some good clothes in his car. I told him to get washed and change into them, while I fixed things up with Danny. "And hurry," I said, as he hesitated. "Get back here as fast as you can. You can't keep a high class girl like her waiting."

He snapped out of it, and hurried away.

I went down to the dressing room.

She was waiting there, sullen and defiant and a little afraid. I hadn't told her she could go to her cottage, so she waited. I looked at her sorrowfully, slowly shaking my head.

"Well, you really tore it that time, sister," I said. "You know who that guy was? Just about the richest man in this county. Owns most of the beach property around here. Has a big piece of this pavilion, as a matter of fact."

"I'll bet!" she said—but a trifle uncertainly. "Oh, sure."

"How did Pete Pavlov stack up to you?" I said. "Hardly a fashion-plate, huh? You just can't figure these local people that way, baby. They keep right on working after they get it. They don't go in for show while they're working."

She studied my face uncertainly, trying to read it. I took

her by the elbow and led her to the window. "Who does that guy look like down there?" I said; for Ralph was just taking his clothes out of the Mercedes. "What do you think a buggy like that costs? You think an ordinary janitor would be driving it?"

She stiffened slightly; hell, that Mercedes even bowls me over. Then she shrugged with attempted indifference. So what, she asked. What did it mean to her if he was loaded.

"Just thought you'd like to know," I said. "Just thought you might like to meet him. He could do a lot for a gal if he took the notion to."

"Uh-huh," she said. "You just want to help me, I suppose! You're doing *me* favors!"

"Suit yourself." I picked up my shirt and began putting it on. "It's entirely up to you, baby. You do a little thinking, though, and maybe you'll remember me doing you a favor or two before. It maybe'll occur to you that I can't be any harder on you than I am on myself, and it ain't making me a penny."

"All right!" she snapped. "What do you want me to do about it? I've tried to thank you! I've—I've—"

"Never mind," I said. "I'm satisfied just to see you get ahead. That's all I've ever wanted."

I finished buttoning my shirt. I tucked the tails in, studying her out of the corner of my eye.

She was wavering—teetering one way, then the other. Wavering and then convinced, like the stupid moronic tramp she was. There was nothing in her head. Only in her throat.

And you could dump a thousand gallons of vinegar down it, and she'd still expect the next cup to be lemonade.

"Well," she said. "He did seem awfully nice. I mean, I couldn't tell what he looked like much, but he acted nice and respectful. And—and he clapped for me."

"He's a wonderful guy," I said. "One of the best."

"Well . . . well, I guess I ought to apologize, anyway," she said. "I ought to do that, even if he was only a janitor."

She preceded me up the steps. She started to open the

door that leads out to the bandstand, and suddenly I put out my hand.

"Danny. Wait . . . baby."

It was the way I said it, the last word. A way I'd never thought I could say it. To her. She froze in her tracks, one foot on one step, the other, the shorts drawn high and tight upon her thighs. Then, her head moved and she looked slowly over her shoulder.

"W-what?" she stammered. "What did you cal—say?"

"Nothing," I said. "I guess I . . . nothing."

"Tell me," she said. "Tell me what you want, Rags."

"I want," I said. "I want . . ."

The unobtainable, that was all. The nonexistent. The that which never-would-be. I wanted it and I did not want it, for once achieved there would be nothing left to live for.

"I want you to get your butt out of my face," I said. "Fast. Before I kick it off of you."

IV

Bobbie Ashton

I FINISHED AT the Thorncastle estate about four-thirty in the afternoon, and Mr. Thorncastle—that fine, democratic fat-bottomed man—paid me off personally.

My bill came to twelve dollars. I looked at him from under my lashes as he paid it, and he added an extra five. Managing to stroke my hand in the process. He is a very juicy-looking character, this Thorncastle. I had some difficulty in getting away from him without kicking him in the groin.

Father was already at the table when I reached home. I washed hastily and joined him, begging his pardon for keeping him waiting. He snatched up his fork. Then he slammed it down, and asked me just how long I intended to keep up this nonsense.

"The yard work?" I said. "Why, permanently, perhaps. It would seem well suited to my station in life—you know, with so much racial discrimination—and—"

"Stop it!" His face whitened. "Don't ever let me hear you—"

"—and there's the money," I said. "A chance to advance myself financially."

"Like Ralph Devore, I suppose! Like the town oddjobs man!"

I shrugged. The facts of the matter were under his nose even if he, like the rest of the town, was too dullwitted to see them. Ralph had earned approximately twenty-eight hundred dollars a year for the past twenty-two years. He had spent practically nothing. Ergo, he now had a minimum of fifty thousand dollars, and probably a great deal more.

He had it. He would have to. And now that his income was cut off, he would be worried frantic. For fifty thousand would not represent enough security to Ralph. Not fifty thousand or a hundred thousand. He would visualize its disappearing, vanishing into nothingness, before his life span had run. He would be terrified, and his terror must certainly react terrifyingly upon Luane.

I wondered where he had hidden the money, since, naturally, he had hidden it—how else could he keep its possession a secret?—as, in his insecurity, he would feel that he had to.

Well, no matter where it was now. There was still this first stage of the game to play. When it was played out, I would concentrate on the money—locate and appropriate it. And watch what happened to Luane, then.

She had behaved very badly, Luane. She had made the serious mistake of telling the truth.

That was unfair; it was theft. The truth was mine—I had earned it painfully and it belonged to me. And now, after years of waiting and planning, it was worthless. A heap of rust, instead of the stout, sharp-pronged lever I was entitled to.

What good was the truth, now? How could I use it on *him*, now?

Not much. Not enough. Not nearly enough.

He was talking again, bumbling on with his nonsense about my returning to school whether I thought I was or not.

"You're going, understand? You're going to complete

your education. You can finish up your high school here, or you can go away. And then you're going on to—"

"Am I?" I said.

"You certainly are! Why—what kind of a boy are you? Letting some gossips, some fool woman spoil your life! No one believes anything she says."

"Oh, yes, they do," I said. "Yes, they do, father. I could name at least three who do, right here in our own household."

He stared at me, his mouth trembling, the mist of fear and frustration in his eyes. I winked at him, hoping he would start blubbering. But of course he didn't. He has too much pride for that—too much dignity. Ah, what a proud, upright man my father is!

"You have to leave," he said slowly. "You must see that you have to leave this town. With your mind—with no outlet for your intelligence . . ."

"I'll think about it," I said. "I'll let you know what I decide."

"I said you'd leave! You'll do what I say!"

"I'll tell you what I'll do," I said. "Exactly, dear father, as I damned please. And if what pleases me doesn't please you, you know what you can do about it."

He stood up, abruptly, flinging his napkin to the table. He said, yes, he confounded well *did* know what he could do; and he'd just about reached the point where he was ready to do it.

"You mean you'd call in the authorities?" I said. "I'd hate to see you do that, father. I'd feel forced to go into the background of my supposed incorrigibility, and the result might be embarrassing for you."

I gave him a sunny smile. He whirled, and stamped away to his office.

He was back a moment later, his hat on, his medicine kit in one hand.

"Do one thing, at least," he said. "For your own good. Stay away from that Pavlov girl."

"Myra? Why should I stay away from her?" I said.

"Stay away from her," he repeated. "You know what Pete Pavlov's like. If—if you—he—"

"Yes?" I said. "I'm afraid I don't understand. What possible objection could Pavlov have to his daughter's going about with Doctor Ashton's well-bred, brilliant and, I might add, handsome son?"

"Please, Bob—" His voice sagged tiredly. "Please do it. Leave her alone."

I hesitated thoughtfully. After a long moment, I shrugged.

"Well, all right," I said. "If it means that much to you."

"Thank you. I—"

"I'll leave her alone," I said, "whenever I get ready to. Not before."

He didn't flinch or explode, much to my disappointment. Apparently he'd been partially prepared for the trick. He simply stared at me, hard-eyed, and when he spoke his voice was very, very quiet.

"I have one more thing to say," he said. "A considerable quantity of narcotics is missing from my stock. If I discover any further shortages, I'll see to it that you're punished— imprisoned or institutionalized. I'll do it regardless of what it does to me."

He turned and left.

I scraped up the dishes and carried them out into the kitchen.

Hattie was at the stove, her back turned to me. She stiffened as I went in, then turned part way around, trying to keep an eye on me while appearing occupied with her work.

Hattie is probably thirty-nine or forty now. She isn't as pretty as I remember her as a child—I thought she was the loveliest woman in the world then—but she is still something to take a second look at.

I put the dishes in the sink. I moved along the edge of the baseboard, smiling to myself, watching her neck muscles tighten as I moved out of her range of vision.

I was right behind her before fear forced her to whirl around. She pressed back against the stove, putting her hands out in a pushing-away gesture.

"Why, mother," I said. "What's the matter? You're not afraid of your own darling son, are you?"

"Go 'way!" Her eyes rolled whitely. "Lea' me alone, you hear?"

"But I just wanted a kiss," I said. "Just a kiss from my dear, sweet mother. After all, I haven't had one now, since —well, I was about three, wasn't I? A very long time for a child to go without a kiss from his own mother. I remember being rather heartbroken when—"

"D-don't!" she moaned. "You don't know nothin' about —Get outta here! I tell doctor on you, an' he—"

"You mean you're not my mother?" I said. "You're truly not?"

"N-no! I tol' you, ain't I? Ain't nothin', nobody! I—I—"

"Well, all right." I shrugged. "In that case . . ."

I grabbed her suddenly, clamped her against me, pinning her arms to her sides. She gasped, moaned, struggled futilely. She didn't, of course, cry out for help.

"How about it," I said, "as long as you're not my mother. Keep it all in the family, huh? What do you say we—"

I let go of her, laughing.

I stepped back, wiping her spittle from my face.

"Why, Hattie," I said. "Why on earth did you do a thing like that? All I wanted was— What?" My heart did a painful skip-jump, and there was a choking lump in my throat. "What? I don't believe I understood you, Hattie."

She looked at me, lips curled back from her teeth. Eyes narrowed, steady, with contempt. With something beyond contempt, beyond disgust and hatred.

"You hear' me right," she said. "You couldn' do nothin'. Couldn' an' never will."

"Yes?" I said. "Are you very sure of that, my dearest mother?"

"Huh! Me, I tell *you*." She grinned a skull's grin. "Yeah, I ver' sure, aw right, my deares' son."

"And it amuses you," I said. "Well, I'll tell you, mother. Doubtless it is very funny, but I don't believe we'd better have any further displays of amusement. Not that I'd mind killing you, you understand. In fact, I'll probably get around to that eventually. But I have other projects afoot at the moment—more important projects, if I may say so without hurting your feelings—"

She moved suddenly, made a dash for her room. I followed her—it adjoins the kitchen—and leaned absently against the door. The locked door to my mother's room.

The door that had been locked for . . .

Yes, my recollection was right; it is always right. I had been about three the last time she had kissed me, the last time she had cuddled, babied, mother-and-babied me. I would have remembered it, even if I did not have almost total recall. For how could one forget such a fierce outpouring of love, the balm-like, soul-satisfying warmth of it?

Or forget its abrupt, never-to-be-again withdrawal?

Or the stupid, selfish, cruel bewildering insistence that it had never been?

I was a very silly little boy. I was a very foolish, bad little boy, and I had better pray God to forgive me. I was not sweets or hon or darlin' or even Bobbie. I was Mister Bobbie—Master Robert. Mistah—Mastah Bobbie, a reborn stranger among strangers.

My continuing illnesses? Psychosomatic. The manifold masques of frustration.

My intelligence? Compensatory. For certainly I inherited none from either of them.

I listened at night, when they thought I was asleep. I asked a few questions, strategically spacing them months apart.

She'd had a child; she'd had to wet-nurse me. Where was that child? Dead? Well, where and when had he died? When and where had my mother died?

It was ridiculously simple. Only a matter of putting a few questions to a fatuous imbecile—my father—and an over-sexed docile moron, my mother. And listening to them at night. Listening and wanting to shriek with laughter.

He'd be ruined if anyone found out. It would ruin my life, wreck all my chances.

It would be that way *if*. And what way did the blind, stupid, silly son-of-a-bitch think it was now? What worse way could it be than as it was now?

And, no, it did not need to be that way. Needn't and wouldn't have been for a man with courage and honesty and decency.

I had deduced the truth by the time I was five. Several years later, when I was able to be up and around—to post and receive letters secretly—I proved my deductions.

He, my father, had practiced in only one other state before coming to this one. It had no record of a birth to Mrs. James Ashton, or of the death of said Mrs. Ashton. There was, however, a record of the birth of a son to one Hattie Marie Smith (colored, unmarried; initial birth). And the attending physician was Dr. James Ashton.

Well?

Or perhaps I should say *well!*

As a matter of fact, I said goddammit, since the cigarette was scorching my fingers.

I dropped it to the floor, ground it out with my shoe and rapped on my mother's door.

"Mother," I said. "Mammy—" I knocked harder. "You heah me talkin' to you, mammy? Well, you sho bettah answer then, or your lul ol' boy gonna come in theah an' peel that soft putty hide right offen you. He do it, mammy. You knows all about him—doncha?—an' you knows he will. He gonna wait just five seconds, and then he's gonna bus' this heah ol' doah down an' . . ."

I looked at my wristwatch, began counting off the seconds aloud.

The bed creaked, and I heard a muffled croak. A dull, weary sound that was part sigh, part sob.

"Now, that's better," I said. "Listen closely, because this concerns you. It's my plan for finishing you off, you and my dearly beloved father . . . I am going to take you out to some deserted place, and bind you with chains. I shall so chain you that you will be apart from each other, and yet together. Inseparable yet touching. And you shall be stripped to your lustful hides. And in winter I shall douse you with ice-water, and in summer I shall smother you with blankets. And you shall shriek and shiver with the cold, and you shall scream and scorch with the heat. Yet you shall be voiceless and unheard.

"That will go on for seventeen years, mother. No, I'll be fair—deduct a couple of years. Then I'll bring you back here, pile you into bed together, and give you a sample of the hell that could never be hot enough for you. Set you on fire. Set the house on fire. Set the whole goddamned town on fire. Think of it, mammy! The whole population. Whole families, infants, children, mothers and fathers, grandparents and great-grandparents—all burning, all stacked together in lewd juxtaposition. And it shall come to pass, mammy. Yeah, verily. For to each thing there is a season, mammy, and a time—"

She was moaning peculiarly. Keening, I suppose you would say.

I listened absently, deciding that Pete Pavlov should be spared from my prospective holocaust.

No one else. At last, I could think of no one else at the moment. But certainly Pete Pavlov.

It was early, around eight o'clock, when I arrived at the dance pavilion. The bandstand was dark. The ticket booth—where Myra Pavlov serves as cashier—was closed. Only one of the ballroom chandeliers was burning. There was, however, a light in Pete's office. So I vaulted the turnstile, and started across the dance floor.

He was at his desk, counting a stack of bills. I was almost to the doorway when he looked up, startled, his hand darting toward an open desk drawer.

Then he saw it was I and he let out a disgusted grunt.

"Damn you, Bobbie. Better watch that sneakin' up on people. Might get your tail shot off."

I laughed and apologized. I said I hoped that if anyone ever did try to hold him up, he wouldn't try to stop them.

"You do, huh?" he said. "How come you hope that?"

"Why—why, because." I frowned innocently. "You have robbery insurance, haven't you? Well, why risk your life for some insurance company?"

I suspect, from the brief flicker in his eyes, the very slight change in facial expression, that he had entertained some such notion himself—that is, I should say, a fake robbery to collect on his insurance. He needed money, popular opinion notwithstanding. A robbery would be the simplest, most straightforward means of getting it. And he was a simple (I use the term flatteringly) straightforward man.

I would have been glad to help him perpetrate such a robbery. Broadly speaking, I would have done anything I could to help him. Unfortunately, however—although I respected him for it—he distrusted me instinctively.

So he treated me to a long, unblinking gaze. Then he grunted, spat in the spittoon and leaned back in his chair. He rocked back and forth in it, hands locked behind his head, looking down at the desk and then slowly raising his eyes to mine.

"I tell you," he said. "Used to be a hound dog around these parts. Fast-footedest goddamned dog you ever saw in your life. You know what happened to him?"

"I imagine he ran over himself," I said.

"Yup. Bashed his brains out with his own butt. Hell of a nice-looking dog, too, and he seemed smart as turpentine. Always wondered why he didn't know better'n to do a thing like that."

I smiled. Pete would not have wondered at all about the why of his allegorical dog. Nor the why of anything. Like myself, Pete's concern was with what things were, not how or why they had become that way.

He finished counting the money. He put it in a tin cash box, locked it up in his safe and came back to the desk. Sat down on a corner of it in front of me, one thick leg swung over the other.

"Well—" His hard, hazel-colored eyes rolled over on my face. "Figure on sleepin' in here tonight? Want me to move you in a bed?"

"I'm sorry." I got up reluctantly. "I was just—uh—"

"Yeah? Something on your mind?"

"N-no. No, I guess not," I said. "I just dropped by to say hello. I didn't have anything to do for a while, so I—"

He looked at me steadily. He spat at the spittoon without shifting his eyes. I cleared my throat, feeling a hot, embarrassing flush spread over my face.

He stood up suddenly, and started for the door. Spoke over his shoulder, his voice gruff.

"Ain't got nothing to do myself for a few minutes. Come on and I'll buy you a sody."

I followed him to a far corner of the ballroom; followed, since he kept a half-pace in front of me. I wanted to pay for the drinks, but he brushed my hand aside, dropped two dimes into the Coke machine himself.

He handed me a bottle. I thanked him and he grunted, jerking the cap on his own.

We stood facing the distant bandstand where the musicians were arriving. We stood side by side, almost touching each other. Separated by no more than a few inches—and silence.

He finished his drink, smacked his lips and dropped the bottle into the empty case. I finished mine reluctantly, disposed of the bottle as he had.

"Well . . ." He spoke as I straightened from the case; spoke, still looking out across the ballroom. "You and Myra steppin' out again tonight?"

I said, why, yes, we were. As soon as she got off work, that is. And after a moment, I added, "If that's all right with you, Mr. Pavlov."

"Know any reason why it shouldn't be?"

"Why—well, no," I said. "I guess not. I mean—"

"I'll tell you," he said. He hesitated, and belched. "I ain't got a goddamned bit of use for you. Never have had, far back as I can remember. But I guess you already know that?"

"Yes," I said. "And I can't tell you how sorry I am, Mr. Pavlov."

"Can't say I'm not sorry myself. Always rather like some-one than dislike 'em." He belched again, mumbling some-thing about the gas. "On the other hand, I got no real reason not to have no use for you. Nothing I can put my finger on. You've always been friendly and polite around me. I don't know of no dirty deals you've pulled, unless'n it's this stuff with Ralph, and I can't really call that dirty, considering. Might've gone off sideways like that myself when I was your age."

"I knew you'd understand," I said. "Mr. Pavlov, I—"

"I was sayin'—" He cut me off curtly. "I got no reason to feel like I do, and reasons are all I go by. People don't give me no trouble, I don't give them any. I rock along with 'em as long as they rock with me. And whether I like 'em or not don't figure in the matter. All right. I guess we understand each other. Now, I got to get busy."

He nodded curtly, and headed back toward his office.

I moved toward the exit.

Myra had come in while Pete and I were talking, and she called to me from the ticket booth. I looked her way blindly, my eyes stinging, misting. Not really hearing or seeing her. I went out without answering her, and sat down in my car.

I got a cigarette lighted. I took a few deep puffs, forcing away my disgusting self-pity. Recovering some of my nor-mal objectiveness.

Pete detested me. It was fitting that he should—things being as they were. And I would not have had it any other way—things being as they were.

But what a pity, what a goddamned pity that they were that way! And why couldn't they have been another, the right and logical way?

Why couldn't my own dear father and mother, those en-cephalitic cretins, those gutless Jukesters those lubricous lusus naturae—why couldn't they have had Myra inflicted upon them? Why should Pete have to suffer such a drab spiritless wretch as she? Why couldn't *they* have had her, and why couldn't he have had—

Myra. A feeling of fury came over me every time I looked

at her. I'd had some plans for her—vague but decidedly unpleasant—long before she came to the office that day a couple of months ago.

Father was away on some calls. I glanced at the notes on her file card.

This was her second trip. She was having menstrual difficulties—something that a good kick in the stomach or a dose of salts would have jarred her out of. But father, that wise and philanthropic Aesculapian, had set her up for a series of hormone shots.

She said she was in a hurry, so I prepared to administer the medication.

Yes, I do that: take care of routine patients. Rather, I did do it, until father became wary. I know a hell of a lot more about medicine than he does. A hell of a lot more about everything than he does. In this case, for example, I knew that what Myra needed—deserved—was not hormone.

I gave her a hypodermic. She "flashed"—to use the slang expression; barely made it to the sink before she started vomiting. I told her it was perfectly all right, and gave her another shot.

Well, someone like that, someone with only part of a character, is made for the stuff. The stuff is made for them. She was hooked in less than a week. She doesn't go to father any more, but she does come to me.

I "treat" her now. I give her what she needs—and deserves. When I am ready to. And after certain ceremonies.

Ten-thirty came. Not more than five minutes later, which was as fast as she could make it, she was running toward the car. Begging before she had the door open.

I told her to shut up. I said that if she said one more word until I gave her permission, she would get nothing.

I had her well trained. She subsided, mouth twisting, gulping down the whimpers that rose in her throat.

I drove to a place about six miles up the beach—Happy Hollow, it is called, for reasons which you may guess. I suppose there is some such place in every community, dubbed with the same sly euphemism or a similar one.

It—this place—was not a hollow; not wholly, at least. Most of its area was hill, wooded and brushy, marked with innumerable trails and side-trails which terminated in tire-marked, beach-like patches of sand.

I stopped at one of these patches. The only tire-marks were those of my own car.

I made her take her clothes off. I grabbed her. I shook her and slapped her and pinched her. I called her every name I could think of.

She didn't speak or cry out. But suddenly I stopped short, and gave her the shot. I was tired. There seemed no point in going on. Action and words, words and action—leading to nothing, arriving nowhere. It wasn't enough. There can be no real satisfaction without an objective.

Myra lay back in the seat, breathing in long deep breaths, eyes half shut. She didn't have a bad shape. In fact, without clothes on—she simply couldn't wear clothes—she shaped up quite beautifully. But only aesthetically, as far as I was concerned. I felt no desire for her.

I wanted to. My mind shrieked that I should. But the flesh could not hear it.

She dozed. I may have dozed myself, or perhaps I merely became lost in thought. At any rate, I snapped back to awareness suddenly, aroused by the dull lacing of light through the trees, the throb of a familiar motor.

Myra sat up abruptly. Stared at me, eyes wide with fright. I told her to sit still and be quiet. Just do what I told her to, and she'd be all right.

I listened to the motor, following the progress of the car. It stopped, with a final purring *throb-throb*, and I knew exactly where it had stopped.

I hesitated. I opened the door of the car.

"B-Bobbie . . ." A frightened whisper from Myra. "Where you going? I'm afraid to stay—"

I told her to shut up; I'd only be gone for a few minutes.

"B-but why? What're you going to—?"

"Nothing. I don't know. I mean—hell, just shut up!" I said.

I went down the trail a few yards. I branched off into another, and then another. I came to the end of it—near the end of it, and hunkered down in the shadows of the trees.

They weren't more than twenty feet away, Ralph Devore and that what's-her-name—the girl with the orchestra. I could see them clearly in the filtered moonlight. I could hear every word they said, every sound. And the way it looked and sounded . . .

I could hardly believe it, particularly of a guy like Ralph. Because when Ralph stepped out with 'em, it was for just one thing and he lost no time about getting it. Yet now with this girl—and, no, she certainly didn't hate him. She obviously felt the same way about him that he did her, and that way—

I didn't know what it was for a moment. Then, when I finally knew—remembered—realized—I refused to admit it. I grinned to myself, silently jeering them, jeering myself. Ralph was really making time, I thought. Here it was only the sixth week of the season, he'd only known this babe six weeks, and they were cutting up like a couple of newlyweds. Newlyweds, sans the sex angle. Which, of course, they'd soon be getting around to.

Maybe—I thought—I ought to do the silly jerk a favor. Go up to his house some night and bump off Luane. It could be made to look like an accident. And believe me, it would need to look damned little like one to leave Ralph in the clear. Father was the coroner, the county medical officer. As for the county attorney, Henry Clay Williams . . . I shook my head, choking back a laugh. You had to hand it to that goddamned Luane. She had a positively fiendish talent for tossing the knife, for plunging it into exactly the right spot to send the crap flying. Henry Clay Williams was a bachelor. Henry Clay Williams lived with his maiden sister. And Henry Clay Williams' sister had an abdominal tumor . . . which created a bulge normally created by a different kind of growth.

At any rate, and unless the job was done in front of witnesses, it would be ridiculously easy to get away with killing

Luane. Just make it look like an accident, enough like one to give Brother Williams an out, and—

I leaned forward, straining to hear them, Ralph and the girl, for they were clinging even closer to each other than they had been, and their voices were consequently muffled:

"Don't you worry one bit, honey"—her. *"I don't know how, but—but gosh, there's got to be some way! I just love you so much, and you're so wonderful and—"*

"Not wonderful 'nough for you"—him. Old love-'em-and-scram Ralph, for God's sake! Why, he sounded practically articulate. *"Ain't it funny, sweetheart? Here I am an old man—"*

"You are not! You're the sweetest, darlingest, kindest, handsomest . . ."

"Anyways, I mean I lived all these years, and I reckon I never knew there was such a thing. Like love I mean. I guess I . . ."

I found that I was smiling. I scrubbed it away with my fist, scrubbed my eyes with my fist. But it kept coming back. That word, the one he'd spoken, the one I'd been ducking—it kept coming back. And I knew that there was no other word for what this was.

He wasn't going to pitch it to her. She wasn't going to hit him up for dough. They were in love—*ah, simply, simply in love! Only—only!*—in love. And, ah, the sweetness of it, the almost unbearable beauty and wonderment of it.

To be loved like that! More important, to love like that!

I smiled upon them, at them. Smiled like a loving god, happy in their happiness. Probably, I thought, I should kill them now. It would be such a wonderful way—time—to die.

I glanced around absently. I ran a hand back under the bushes, searching for a suitable club or rock. I could find none—nothing that would do the job with the instantaneousness necessary, nothing that was sufficiently sturdy or heavy.

I did locate a pointed, dagger-like stick, and I considered it for a moment. But a very little mental calculation established that it would never do. It wasn't long enough. It would never pass through the barrel-chest of Ralph's and go on into her bosom. And if I did not get them both at the same time, if I left one to live without the other—!

I almost wept at the thought.

A strange warmth spread over me. Spread down from my head and up from my feet. It increased, intensified, and I did not know what it was. How could I, never having experienced it before? And then at last I knew, and I knew what had brought it about.

I straightened up. I backed down the trail quietly, and then I turned and strode toward my car excitedly, my mind racing.

There could be nothing now, of course. Dope inhibits the sexual impulses, so she would have to be tapered off first. But that should be relatively easy; she should unhook almost as easily as she had been hooked. If I could just get the stuff to work with—and I *would* get it, by God! I'd kill that stupid son-of-a-bitch, my father, if he gave me any trouble . . .

I cut off the thought. Somehow the thought of parricide, entirely justifiable though it was, interfered with the other.

I would get what I needed in some way. That was all that mattered. And meanwhile I could be preparing her, laying the necessary groundwork. And meanwhile I *knew*.

I KNEW!

I reached the car. I climbed in, smiling.

She had her coat draped over her, but she was still undressed. I told her, lovingly, to get dressed, Lovingly, with tender pats and caresses, I started to help her.

"D-don't . . . !" She shivered. "What d-do you want?"

"Nothing," I said. "Only what you want, darling. Whatever you want, that's what I want."

She stared at me like a snake-charmed bird. Her teeth chattered. I took her in my arms, gently pressed my mouth against hers. I smiled softly, dreamily, stroking her hair.

"That's all I want, honey," I said. "Now, you tell me what you want."

"I w-want to go home. P-please, Bobbie. Just—"

"Look," I said. "I love you. I'd do anything in the world for you. I—"

I kissed her. I crushed her body against mine. And her lips were stiff and lifeless, and her body was like ice. And the glow was leaving me. The life and the resurrection were leaving me.

"D-don't," I said. "I mean, please. I only want to love you, only to love you and have you love me. That's all. Only sweetness and tenderness and—"

Suddenly I dug my fingers into her arms. I shook her until her silly stupid head almost flopped off.

I told her she'd better do what I said or I'd kill her.

"I'll do it, by God!" I slapped her in the face. "I'll beat your goddamned head off! You be nice to me, you moronic bitch! Be sweet, you slut! Y-you be gentle and tender and loving—you love me, DAMN YOU, YOU LOVE ME! Or I'll . . . I'll . . ."

V

Dr. James Ashton

IT MAY RING false when I say so, but I did love her. Back in the beginning and for several years afterward. It became impossible later on, will it as I would and despite anything I could do. For we could share nothing but a bed, and that less and less frequently. We would not share the most important thing we had. It *was* impossible——you see that, do you not? So the love went away.

But once long ago . . .

She was twenty-two or -three when she came to me. She was practically illiterate——a shabby, life-beaten slum-dweller. There was a great deal of race prejudice in that state——there is still, unfortunately, so much everywhere—— and Negroes got little if any schooling; they had no place to live but slums.

I hired her as my housekeeper. I paid her twice the pittance, the prevailing and starvation wage for Negro house-workers. I gave her decent quarters, a clean attic room with a lavatory, there in my own house.

She was thin, undernourished. I saw to it that she got

plenty of good wholesome food. She needed medical attention. I gave it to her—taking time from paying patients to do so.

I shall never forget the day I examined her. I had suspected the beauty of her body, even in the shabby ill-fitting clothes I had first seen her in. But the revelation of it was almost more than the eyes could bear. Of all the nude women I had seen—professionally, of course—I had seen none to compare with her. She was like a statue, sculpted of ivory by one of the great masters. Even frail and half-starved, she—

But I digress.

She was very grateful for all I had done for her. Overflowing with gratitude. Her eyes followed me wherever I went, and in them there was that burning worship you see in a dog's eyes. I think that if I had ordered her to take poison she would have done so instantly.

I did not want her to feel that way. At least, I made it very clear to her that she owed me nothing. I had done no more than was decent, I explained. No more than one decent person should do for another—circumstances permitting. All I wanted of her, I said, was that she be happy and well, as such a fine young woman should be.

She would not have it so. I wanted—was more than willing to, at any rate—but not she. There was an immutable quality about her gratitude. Wherever I was, there was it: quietly omnipotent, passively resistant, a constant proffering. Impossible to dispose of; beyond, at least, my powers.

I did not wish to hurt her feelings. I could see no real harm in accepting what she was so anxious to give. It was all she had to give. And the gift of one's all is not lightly rejected.

Finally, around the middle of her second month of service with me, I accepted it.

There was no love in it that first time. None on my side, that is. It was merely a matter of saving her pride, and, of course—to a degree, at least—physical gratification. But after that, very quickly after that, the love came.

And it was only natural, I suppose, that it should.

I came from a very poor family; migrant sharecroppers. My parents had twelve children—three stillborn, five who died in early childhood. The largest house we ever lived in was two rooms. I was six or seven years old before I tasted cow's milk, or knew that there was such a thing as red meat. I was almost a grown man before I owned a complete set of clothes.

If it had not been for a plantation overseer's taking an interest in me, if he had not induced my father to let me remain with his family when my own moved on, I should probably have wound up like the rest of the brood. Like my living brothers and sisters . . . if they are living. Hoe-hands. Cotton-pickers. White trash.

Or, no, I do myself an injustice. I could never have been like them. I would have found some way to push myself up, overseer or no (and life with him, believe you me, was no bed of roses).

Through grade school, high school, college and medical school—in all that time, I cannot remember having a complete day of rest.

I worked my way every step of the way. I did nothing but work and study. I had no time for recreation, for girls. When I did have the time, when I was at last practicing and reasonably free from financial worry, I had no, well, knack with them. I was ill at ease around girls. I was incapable of the flippery-dippery and chitchat which they seemed to expect. I learned that one young lady I liked—and who, I thought, reciprocated my feeling—had referred to me as a "terrible stick."

So, there you have it. Hattie loved me. A woman more beautiful than any I had ever seen loved me. And I could be with her in the most intimate way—talk to her of the most intimate things (although she could not always answer intelligently)—and feel not a whit of awkwardness.

I fell in love with her deeply. It was inevitable that I should.

I was, of course, quite alarmed when I learned that she

was pregnant. Alarmed and not a little angry. For she had failed to take the precautions I had prescribed and entrusted her to take. As I saw it, there was nothing for it but an abortion, even though she was three months along. But much to my chagrin, for she had always done as I wanted before, Hattie refused.

She was virtually tigerish in her refusal, threatening me with what she would do if I attempted to take the foetus from her. Then as I became firm—considerably shocked by her conduct—she turned to pleading. And I could not help feeling touched, nor the feeling that I had been taken sore advantage of.

The boy (she always spoke of him as a boy) would be able to "pass." After perhaps two hundred years of outrace-breeding, after eight generations, there would be a child of her blood who could pass for white... Couldn' I understand? Didn' I see why she jus' *had* to have it?

I relented. I could have insisted on the abortion, and she would have had to submit. But I did not insist. Except for me, the child would not have been born.

When the pregnancy began to show, I moved her out of the house. From that day on, until she gave birth, I called on her at least twice a week.

I could not go through such an experience now. There were times, even then, when I thought I could stand no more. A white man—*a white doctor!*—visiting in the Negro slums! Treating a Negro woman! It was unheard of, unprecedented—a soul-shaking, pride-trampling experience. White doctors did not treat Negroes. Generally speaking, no one did. They simply did without medical attention, administering to themselves, when it was necessary, with home remedies and patent nostrums; delivering their own babies or depending on midwives.

All in all, they seemed to get by fairly well in that manner —although, Negro vital statistics being what they are, or were, one cannot be sure. And in the good health she was enjoying, I think that Hattie could have gotten by quite well without me. But it apparently didn't occur to her to suggest it. She *didn't* suggest it, anyway; and I hardly felt able to.

For that matter, I don't know that I would have been willing to leave her untended. In fact, and on reflection, I am quite sure that I would not. I was deeply in love with her, deeply concerned for her and our child. Otherwise, I would not have done what I did when the birth became imminent.

Negroes were not treated by white doctors, as I have said. This meant that they were not admitted to white hospitals—and there were nothing but white hospitals. There was a ramshackle, poorly staffed county institution which admitted Negroes, but not unless it was absolutely impelled to. If a Negro was dying he might get in. If he did, he would probably never live to regret it.

Well. I was on the staff of one of the white hospitals. I had only recently obtained the appointment. I got Hattie admitted to it as a white woman, of Spanish-Indian descent.

I did that, knowing almost certainly that the fraud would be discovered. I loved her that much, thought that much of her—and, needless to say, the child.

They were giving her narrow-eyed looks from the moment she stepped through the door. They suspected her from the beginning; me and her. I could see that they did, see it and feel it. Then, when she was coming out of the anaesthesia, when she began to talk...

I shall never forget how they looked at me.

Or what the chief of staff said to me.

I was forced to remove her and the child the following day. I did not put it to an issue—how could I?—but if I had refused to remove them, I believe they would have been thrown out.

That was the end of my staff job, of course. The end of my practice, of everything in that state. Probably I can consider myself lucky that I wasn't lynched.

It was several days before I could nerve myself even to leave the house.

There was only one thing to do: relocate. Move to some place so remote and far away that no word of my secret would ever reach to it. Some place, yes—now that the die was cast—where Hattie could be accepted as my wife.

Down here where we were, they were always on the lookout for colored blood, expert at detecting it. But in a new location—the kind I had in mind—and with a little intensive coaching for Hattie, as to her speech and mannerisms . . . well, my plan seemed entirely feasible.

I believe it would have been, too, if circumstances had not turned out as they did.

I saw a practice advertised here at Manduwoc. I left Hattie and the boy behind, and came here to look at it.

It seemed to fit my needs to a *t*; in remoteness, in distance from that other state. It was not too big a thing financially, the town being as small as it was. But there was a large farm-trade area to draw from, and I was confident that a live-wire could double or even triple the present practice.

I decided to buy it. I went to Henry Clay Williams to have the papers drawn up.

Hank, I should say, was not then the county attorney. He was, in fact, only a few years out of law school. But he was a very shrewd man, very knowing; and he took an immediate liking to me. He looked upon me as a friend, as I did him. He was determined that I should get off on the right foot, and he knew how to go about it.

I owe a lot to Hank. More than any man I know of.

He was very adroit with his advice; he came out with it in a rather backhanded way. He'd lead with a feeler as to my notion on things; then, on the next time around, he'd move in with something a little stronger.

I mustn't think he was nosy, he said. Far be it from him to give a whoop what a man's politics or his religion or his race was. But there were still a hell of a lot of hidebound mossbacks around. People with foolish prejudices—shameful prejudices, in his opinion—although, of course, they had the same right to their ideas that he had to his. And the center of population for those people, by God—Hank gets pretty salty at times—seemed to be right here in Manduwoc!

I laughed. I said it was certainly unfortunate that people had to be that way.

"But what's a man going to do, Jim?" he said. "A man's got a living to make and wants to get somewhere, what can he do about 'em?"

"I guess there's nothing much he can do," I said. "It's a problem of education, evolution. Something that only time can take care of."

"I don't see how he can go around with a chip on his shoulder, do you, Jim?" he said. "Why, look, now. Some of my very best friends are—well, let's say, people that aren't exactly popular around here. My *very* best friends, Jim. But a man can't live off his friends, can he? That wouldn't be fair to them, would it? He has to live with the community as a whole, doesn't he?"

"That's the way it is," I said. "It's too bad, but—"

"It's outrageous," he said. "Absolutely outrageous, Jim. Why, my blood actually boils sometimes at some of the carryings-on in this town. I don't mean that they're not good people, understand? The salt of the earth in many respects. They're just narrow-minded, and they don't want to broaden. And if you try to buck 'em, give 'em the slightest reason to get their claws into you—hell, they don't actually need a real reason, if you know what I mean—why, they'll rip you apart. I've seen it happen, Jim. There's a man here in town, now, a Bohunk contractor name of Pete Pavlov. He . . ."

"I see," I said. "I understand what you mean, Hank."

"And you think I've got the right slant, Jim? You agree with me?"

"Oh, absolutely," I said. "There's no question about it. Now, there is one thing—in view of what you've told me. As I've mentioned, my wife died recently, and—"

"A great loss, I'm sure. My deepest sympathies to you, Jim."

"—and I have our infant son to take care of," I said. "Or, I should say, I have a Ne—nigger woman taking care of him. A wet nurse. I suppose I could get another one for him, but—"

"Oh, well," Hank shrugged. "She's a southern nigger, isn't she? Knows her place? Well, that'll be all right. After all, no one could expect you to take a baby away from its nurse."

"Well, I certainly wouldn't want to," I said.

"And you don't have to. As long as she stays in her place —and I guess you'll see to that, won't you? ha-ha—she'll get along fine."

. . . I don't see how I could have done anything else.

I certainly had no easy row to hoe myself.

It is only in recent years that I have been able to take things a little easy. Before that it was work, work, work, until all hours of the day and night. Fighting to hold on to the old practice, to build it into something really worthwhile. Fighting to be someone, to build something . . . for nothing.

I had no time for them, the boy and her. No time, at least, on many days. Perhaps—to be entirely truthful—I did not want time for them. And if I did not, I hardly see how I can be faulted for it.

It was awkward being with her, even in intimacy. She made me feel uncomfortable, guilty, hypocritical. I had become something here, and I was rapidly becoming more. I was a big frog in a little puddle. A deacon in the church. A director of the bank. A pillar in the community. Yet here I was, sleeping with a Negro wench!

I would have stopped it even if it had not become dangerous. My conscience would not have allowed me to continue.

As for the boy, I did—and do, I am afraid—love him . . . as I did her, so long ago. He was my own flesh and blood, my only son. And I loved him, as I loved her. But like her, although in a different way, he made me uncomfortable. It distressed me to be around him.

I cannot say why, exactly, but I am confident of one thing. It was not a matter of resentment.

I did not blame him, an innocent child, for my own tragic and irremediable error.

* * *

f I could lay the whole truth before him, I might be able to make him understand. But naturally I cannot do that. It is impossible for him to be absolutely sure of the truth. He may guess and suspect and think, but he cannot *know*. He can only know if I admit it, so of course I never will.

Probably, he wouldn't understand, anyway. He wouldn't allow himself to. He is too selfish, too filled with self-pity —yes, despite his arrogant manner. If he understood, he could not play the martyr. He would have no justification for his vileness and viciousness—assuming, that is, that it could be justified. For certainly, whatever I may or may not have done, such conduct could never be justified.

I don't know how such a—a *creature* could be my son.

I don't know what to do about him.

I have no control over him whatsoever. I can't—and he knows I can't—appeal to the authorities for help. And, no, it isn't because of the scandalous, fiendish lies he would tell. I can be hurt by scandal, of course; in fact, I have been hurt. But not greatly. I am too thoroughly entrenched here. Everyone knows too well where Dr. James Ashton stands, and what he stands for.

I have not taken the stringent measures (which I doubtless should have) because I love him. I can't cause him hurt, regardless of how much he deserves it. Also, as you may have surmised, I am afraid of him.

It is a hideous thing to live in terror of one's own son, but I do. I try to keep it concealed, to carry on, to maintain some semblance of father-and-son relationship, but it is becoming increasingly difficult. I am terrified of him, more and more every day. And he is very well aware of the fact. I have the frightful feeling at times that he can read my mind. At times, I am almost sure that he can. He seems to know what I am going to do even before I know it myself. Nonsensical as it sounds, he *does* know. So, I have not taken the steps which I doubtless should have. I have avoided seriously contemplating such steps. He would kill me before I could carry them out.

He is capable of it. He has threatened to—to kill both Hattie and me.

To be fair to him, if that is the right word, he has made no such threats recently. There were occasions recently when I was hopeful that he might be coming to his senses. But . . .

About three weeks ago, I thought I saw signs that he was losing interest in that degrading yard work. He was leaving later in the mornings, returning earlier at night. He apparently felt—I thought—that he had cheapened me all he could by doing such work, and was now on the point of dropping it.

I asked him to do so. "Not on my account," I said. "I know it's useless to appeal to you on those grounds. Just do it for yourself. Just think of what it looks like for a boy of your background, and intelligence to—"

"I'm considering it," he said. "I may possibly do it, if you don't urge me to it."

"Well, that's fine," I said. For, God pity me, there was some comfort—a relative lot—in even such an insolent, heartless reply as that. "You don't have to do that kind of work, or any work. I'll be delighted to give you any money that you need."

"Don't be offensive," he said. "Don't bother me."

He said it quite mildly. I felt considerably encouraged.

Then, I came home the following night to find every drawer, every cabinet, in my office had been opened and rummaged through. No, he hadn't broken them open. He had simply picked all the locks.

Now, he was seated in my chair, his feet up on my desk, absently smoking a cigarette.

I was so angry that for a moment I forgot my terror. I told him that he had better explain himself, and promptly, or he would have serious cause to regret it.

"Where is the stuff?" he said. "In your safety-deposit box?"

"It's where you'll never—what stuff?" I said. "I've warned you, Bobbie, you—"

"I had an idea it was," he nodded. "Well, it looks like I'll just have to buy some."

He got up and started to leave. I grabbed him and whirled him around. "You rotten, filthy scum!" I said. "I'll tell you what you'll do, and what will happen to you if you don't! You'll—"

"Let go of me," he said.

"I'll let go of you! I'll drag you straight down to the courthouse! I'll—"

I let go of him suddenly. The fiendish sadistic whelp had crushed his cigarette into my wrist.

"Don't ever do anything like that again," he said calmly. "Do you understand me, father?"

"Bobbie . . . son," I said. "For God's sake, what do you want? What are you trying to do? That—that girl—"

"Don't interfere with me," he said.

He drove into the city the next day. He has made one other trip in since then. For what purpose, I needn't explain.

How he manages it I don't know. How a seventeen-year-old boy in a strange city can promptly locate a narcotics peddler and make a purchase, I don't know.

Perhaps he doesn't buy it. God—and I know I'm being ridiculous—he may make it! I have an insane notion that he could, if he wanted to. Anything that is mean and vicious, rotten, cruel, filthy, senseless . . . !

He is still doing the yard work, of course. Degrading himself, playing the flunkey, to buy dope for her.

If I could discover his motive, I might be able to do something. But what possible motive could he have? The girl is completely undesirable. As intelligent and handsome as he is, he could have his way with virtually any girl in town, without the deadly risk he is running. For it is a deadly one. It would be so, even without the complication of narcotics. Pete has only to find them together—in a certain way—and that will be the end.

Pete will kill him. Pete might even kill me.

I have almost driven myself crazy wondering what to do,

but I can think of nothing. I can only wait, go on as I always have and wait—watch helplessly while doom approaches.

And Luane is responsible. Bobbie was always somewhat peculiar, withdrawn, but except for that sluttish old hypochondriac it would never have happened.

I broke with her last week. I may have to tolerate him, but I do not have to put up with her.

I told her there was nothing at all wrong with her, that I would not under any circumstances visit her again, that if she wanted a doctor she would have to call another (the nearest is twenty miles away). Then I walked out, leaving her to whine and complain to her own filthy self.

I should have done that long ago. I forebore only because it might seem that I was bothered by her slander, and thus lend weight to it.

Bobbie seemed pleased when I mentioned the matter casually at the dinner table.

"That was very wise of you," he said. "I'd expected you to do it sooner."

"Well," I said, "as a matter of fact, I had been con—"

"But, no, I can see that this way is better," he said. "It eliminates you pretty conclusively from the potential list of suspects. Now, if you'd cut her off sooner, let it be known that you were no longer going near her place *before* you established that you held no grudge against her . . ."

"Stop it!" I said. "What are you talking about, anyway? I refuse to listen to any more such nonsense!"

"Why, of course." He winked at me, grinning. "It isn't very discreet, is it? And we don't need to talk, do we, dear father?"

I have been wondering lately if he is really my son. Wondering idly, wishfully perhaps, but still speculating on the matter. After all, if she would hop into bed with me so quickly, why not with another? How do I know what she was doing during the hours when I was away from the house? Obviously, she was of not much account. A woman who would behave as shamelessly as she did, tempting me until I could withstand it no longer, playing upon my kindness and sense of honor...

Well, never mind. He is my son. I know it. And I would be the last man in the world to attempt to evade my responsibilities. But that changes nothing, as far as she is concerned.

She had better not complain to me any more about Bobbie's abuse. Not one word. Or I personally will give her something to complain about. I would send her packing if I dared to, which regrettably I don't. It would look bad, as though the scandal had hit home. It would look like I was afraid—on the run.

So things stand; to this sorry, unbearable state I have come. Chained to a Negro woman—and I am *not* responsible to her. Inflicted with a son who—who—well, at least he isn't a Negro. Not really. If a Negro was only one-sixteenth white, would you call him a white man? Well, it's the same proposition. It's—

It's unbearable. Maddening. Completely unjust.

I don't know what I would do without the comfort of Hank Williams' friendship. I spend much of my free time with him, and he spends much of his with me. We understand each other. He admires and respects me. He is glad that I have gotten ahead, even though his own success has been somewhat modest. True, he seems unaware that he hasn't gotten on—he seems to have forgotten that he ever talked of being senator or governor. But, no matter. He is my friend, and he has proved it in many ways. If he wishes to be a little smug, boastful, I can bear with it easily. Never in any way do I let on that his "success" wears a striking resemblance to failure.

We were talking the other night about our early days here. And he, as he is wont to do, passed some remark as to his progress since then. I said that his was a career to be proud of, that very few lawyers had risen so high in so brief a time. He beamed and smirked; and then with that earnest warmth which only he is capable of, he said that he owed his success to me.

"Well," I said. "I've certainly boosted you whenever I could, but I'm afraid I—"

"Remember our first talk together? The day I was drawing up those papers for you?"

"Why, yes," I said. "Of course I remember. You set me straight here, saw that—"

"Sure! Uh-hah. You sly old rascal you!" He threw back his head, and laughed. "I set *you* straight. A country bumpkin, a small town lawyer, set a big city doctor straight. He told *him* how to get on in the world!"

I didn't say anything. I was too bewildered. For I had told him nothing that day. Nothing until I had pretty well ascertained his own feelings.

"Oh, I understood you, all right!" he laughed. "Naturally, you couldn't come straight out with it; you had to spar around a little, make sure of how I felt first. But . . ."

He winked at me, grinning. I stared at him, feeling my hands tighten on the arms of my chair; then, as the murderous hatred drained out of me, feeling them slowly relax and grow limp.

He had done me no injury. His intelligence, his moral stamina, that vaguely concrete thing called character—all had been stunted at the outset. Perhaps they would have amounted to little, regardless; perhaps environment and heredity would have dwarfed them, without the withering assistance of our long-ago, initial conversation.

At any rate, he had not harmed me; he had not changed me one whit from what I essentially was. Others, doubtless, many others, but not me.

If anything, it was the other way around.

He was frowning slightly, looking a little uncomfortable and puzzled. He repeated his phrase about my having had to spar around with him, until I was sure of how he felt.

"And how did you feel, Hank?" I said. "Basically—deep down in your heart?"

"Oh, well," he shrugged. "You don't need to ask that, Jim. You know how I stand on those things."

"But back then," I insisted, "right back in the beginning. Tell me, Hank. I really want to know."

"We-el—" He hesitated, and spread his hands. "You know, Jim. About like most people, I guess. A lot of people, anyway. Kind of on the fence, and wishing I could stay there. But knowing I had to jump one way or the other, and knowing I was pretty well stuck on the side I jumped to. I—well, you know what I mean, Jim. It's kind of hard to put into words."

"I see," I said. "I hoped . . . I mean, I thought that was probably the way you felt."

"Well," he said; and, after a moment, again, "Well."

He studied me a trifle nervously; then, unable to read my expression, he gave out with that bluffly amiable, give-me-approval laugh of his.

It was a hearty laugh, but one that he was ready to immediately modulate. His face was flushed with high good humor: a mask of good-fellowship hilarity which could, at the wink of an eye, with practiced effortlessness, become the essence of gravity, sobriety, seriousness.

I laughed along with him. With him, and at myself. Our laughter filled the room, flowed out through the windows into the night; echoing and reechoing, sending endless ripples on and on through the darkness. It remained with us, the laughter, and it departed from us. Floating out across the town, across hill and dale, across field and stream, across mountain and prairie, across the night-lost farm houses, the hamlets and villages and towns, the bustling, tower-twinkling cities. Across—around—the world, and back again.

We laughed, and the whole world laughed.

Or should I say jeered?

Suddenly I got up and went to the window. Stood there unseeing, though my eyes were wider than they had ever been, my back turned to him.

And where there had been uproar, there was now silence. Almost absolute silence.

He could not stand that, of course. After almost twenty years, it dawned on me that he could not. Whenever there is silence, he must fill it. With something. With anything. So, after he had regained his guffaw-drained breath, after he had achieved a self-satisfactory evaluation of my mood, he spoke again. Went back to the subject of our conversation.

"Well, anyway, Jim. As I was saying, I'm eternally grateful to you. I hate to think what might have happened if we hadn't had that talk."

I winced, unable to answer him for a moment. Immediately his voice tightened, notched upward with anxiety.

"Jim . . . Jim? Don't you look at it that way, too, Jim? Don't you kind of hate to think—"

"Oh, yes—" I found my voice. "Yes, indeed, Hank. On the other hand . . ."

"Yeah? What were you going to say, Jim?"

"Nothing," I said. "Just that I doubt that it would have changed anything. Not with men like us."

VI

Marmaduke "Goofy" Gannder (Incompetent)

When I awakened it was morning, and I was lying on the green pavement of The City of Wonderful People, and a hideous hangover held me in its thrall.

I sat up by degrees, shaking and shuddering. I massaged my eyes, wondering, yea, even marveling, over the complete non-wonderment of the situation. For lo! I invariably have a hangover in the morning, even as it is invariably morning when I awaken: and likewise, to complete the sequence of non-marvelousness, I invariably awaken in The City of Wonderful People.

"Hell," I thought (fervently); "the same today, yesterday and—*Ouch!*"

I said the last aloud, adding a prayerful expletive, for the sunlight had stabbed into my eyes, speared fierily into my head like a crown of thorns. In my agony, I rocked back and forth for a moment; and then I staggered to my feet and stumbled over to Grandma's bed.

It was not a very nice bed, compared to those of the City's other inhabitants. Untended, except for my inept ministrations, it was protected only by an oblong border of wine bottles, which seemed constantly to be getting broken. And it was sunken in uncomfortably: and the grass was withered and brown—yeah, generously fertilized as it obviously was by untold numbers of dogs, cats and rodents. The headboard of the bedstead was of weathered, worm-eaten wood, a dwarfed phallus-like object bearing only her name and the word "Spinster": painfully, or perhaps, painlessly, free of eulogy.

I studied the bleak inscription, thinking, as I often do when not occupied with other matters, that I should do something about it. I had considered substituting the words "Human Being," with possibly a suffixed "Believe It Or Not." But Grandma had not liked that: she had considered it no compliment. And she had made no bones—no pun intended—about letting me know it.

I sat facing her bed, my head bowed against the sun, staring down into the sunken hummock. The grass rustled restlessly, whispering in the wind; and after a time there was a dry, snorting chuckle.

"Well?" Grandma said. "Penny for your thoughts."

"Now, that—" I forced a smile. "Now, that is the sort of thing that brings on inflation."

Grandma snickered. She asked me how I was getting along with my book.

I said fine, that, in fact, I had finished it.

"Well, let's hear some of it," Grandma said. "Start right with the beginning."

"Certainly, Grandma," I said. "Certainly . . . 'Once upon a time, there were two billion and a half bastards who lived in a jungle, which weighed approximately six sextillion, four hundred and fifty quintillion short tons. Though they were all brothers, these bastards, their sole occupation was fratricide. Though the jungle abounded in wondrous fruits, their sole food was dirt. Though their potential for knowledge was unlimited, they knew but one thing. And what they knew was only what they did not know. And what they did not know was what was enough.'"

I stopped speaking.

Grandma stirred impatiently. "Well, go on."

"That's all there is," I said.

"But I thought you said you'd finished. That's no more than you had before."

"It's all there is," I repeated. "As I see it, there is nothing more to say."

We were silent for a time. Without talk to divert me, my hangover began to return, crept slowly up through my body and over my head. Shaking me, sickening me, gnawing at me inside and out like some hateful and invisible reptile.

Grandma snickered sympathetically. "Pretty sick, aren't you?"

"A little," I said. "Something I took internally seems to have disagreed with me. Or, I should say—in all fairness— I disagreed with it. It was entirely friendly and tractable until I removed it from the bottle."

"You know what to do about it," Grandma said. "You know what you've got to do."

"I don't know whether I can make it," I said. "Rather, I have a strong suspicion that I can't make it."

"You've got to," Grandma said, "so stop wasting good breath. Stop talking and start moving."

I groaned piteously, making futile motions of arising. The flesh was willing, but also weak. And as for spirit, I had none whatsoever.

"Verily, Grandma," I moaned. "Verily, verily. I would swap my soul to Satan for one good drink."

"Cheapskate," said Grandma. "Now, cut out the gab and get on your way."

I nodded miserably. Somehow, I managed to get to my feet. "I shall do as you say, Grandma," I said.

Grandma made no reply. Presumably she had returned to her well-earned sleep.

I turned and tried to tiptoe away from her. I lost my balance and fell flat on my face, and minutes passed before I could pick myself up again. Finally after several similar fallings and pickings-up, I reached the road to town.

A truck was coming from the opposite direction. It looked like Joe Henderson's, and it was. I swung an arm, limply, thumb upraised, in the gesture as old as hitchhiking. Joe slowed down, and came to a stop. Then, as I reached for the door, he jabbed one finger into the air, and roared away.

I walked on, more strengthened, more firm in my purpose than otherwise. I wondered what loss Joe could suffer that could not be recouped by insurance, and I decided that the tires of his truck would be a very good bet.

Another farm truck drove up behind me—Dutch Eaton's. Dutch stopped and leaned out, asked me solicitously if I was tired of walking.

"Yes," I said, "but please spare me the suggestion that I run a while. It was not very amusing even when I first heard it, back during my cradle days."

His fat face reddened with anger. He sputtered, "Why, you crazy, low-down—!"

"Listen," I said. "Listen, listen, Mr. Eaton. What is it that is gutless, brainless and moves around on wheels? A swine, Mr. Eaton. A pig in overalls."

He had been easing the door open. Now, he sprang out with a furious roar, and, whirling, I also sprang. I am almost always equal to such emergencies. Weak though I may have been a moment before, the strength and the agility to save myself invariably come to me. And they did now.

So I leaped the ditch, and vaulted easily over the fence. I walked on up into the orchard in the rear of the Devore estate, listening to Dutch curse me, and, finally, drive away.

Temporarily, I was so absorbed in thought that I almost forgot my hangover. In a sense, I had reason to be grateful to Dutch Eaton and Joe Henderson. Yet I must confess that the emotion I felt for them was very far from gratitude.

Joe and Dutch, I thought. They had been on bad terms with one another for years. What would be the result, say, if Joe's tires should be slashed on the same night that Dutch's barn burned down?

"Lord World forgive me," I murmured, "for their minds are even as those of a Paleolithic foetus, and I know all too damned well what I do."

I had passed through the orchard by now, and arrived at the barnyard. Moving boldly but quietly, I went through the gate, crossed the barnyard and backyard, and entered the back door of the house.

No, there was no danger. I knew that, having visited the place several times before, Ralph would be away. Luane would be in bed, and her bedroom was on the front. As long as I was quiet, and no one can be more quiet than I, I could prowl the downstairs at will.

I stopped inside the door a moment, listening. Faintly, from upstairs, Luane's voice drifted down to me as she talked over the telephone:

". . . course, I hate to say anything either. Far be it from me to say a word about anyone, and you know it, Mabel. But a thing like that—a young girl lifting her skirts for a nigger—and that father of hers, always acting so high and mighty. . ."

I hesitated, feeling vaguely impelled to do something. Knowing that if anything could ever have been done, it was too late now. Pete Pavlov would soon hear the gossip. As soon as he ascertained its truth, he would act. And there could be no doubt about how he would act—what he would do.

I frowned, shrugged, and pushed the matter out of my mind; mentally disconnecting the vicious whine of Luane's voice. I could not help the inevitable. On the other hand, I hoped, I could help myself to a drink; and my need for one was growing.

I opened the cupboard, a familiar section of it. I studied the several bottles of flavoring extract, my mouth watering. And then miserably, having noted the labels, I turned away. There was no end, apparently, to Ralph's skimping. Since my last visit, he had substituted cheap, nonalcoholic extracts for the fine, invigorating brands he had previously stocked.

I looked through the other cupboards. I hesitated over a

large bottle of floor polish: then, insufficiently intrigued by its five per cent alcoholic content, I turned away again. Finally, I lifted a trap door in the floor, and went down into the cellar.

I had no luck there, either. Ralph's cider was freshly made—still sweet; and he had done his canning as expertly as he did everything else. Out of all the endless jars of fruit and vegetables, there was not a one that was beginning to ferment.

I went back up into the kitchen. Sweat pouring off of me, my nerves screaming for the balm of drink. I went through the connecting door to the front hall, and stood at the foot of the stairs.

There would be plenty to drink up there. Rubbing alcohol. Female tonic. Liniment. Perhaps even something that was made to be drunk. And if Luane would only go to sleep, if she would cease her poisonous spewing for only a few minutes . . .

But, obviously, she would not. Already she had another party on the wire, and when she had finished with that one she would immediately ring up another. And so on throughout the day. She would never stop—unless she was stopped. As well she deserved to be, aside from my crying need. But I could not envision myself now in the role of stopper, and being unable to I could not act as such.

Another day, perhaps. Some other day, or night, when thirst and hopelessness brought me here again.

I left the house. I retraced my steps through the orchard, and walked toward town, turning eventually into the alley that ran behind Doctor Ashton's house.

Doctor Ashton would not be at home at this hour, nor would he assist me if he was. As for his son, Bobbie, who doubtless was also away, I had accepted his help but once, and that once was more than enough. I still shuddered when I recalled the experience. What he gave me, that angel-faced phlegmatic fiend, I do not know. But it practically removed my bowels, and nausea shook me like a terrier-shaken rat for the ensuing three days.

I could look for nothing, then, from Ashton or his son. But the Negro woman, Hattie, would be at home, she never went anywhere. And doubtless out of superstition—a kind of awe of the so-called insane—she had given me drink several times in the past.

I knocked on the back door. There was a *sluff-sluff* of house slippers, and then she was standing at the screen, looking out at me dully.

"Go 'way," she said, before I could speak. "Go 'way and stay 'way. Don't want no more truck with you."

I read the tone of her voice, the reason behind her attitude. At least, I believe I did. I told her she was completely mistaken if she believed I was bad luck.

"Listen, listen, Miss Hattie," I said. "You see this caul in my left eye? Now, I'm sure you know that a man with a caul in his eye—"

"I knows you an' 'at eye bettah be moving," she said. "You an' it want to go on keepin' company. Get now, you heah me? Get along, crazy man!"

"Please," I said. "Please do not refer to me as crazy. I have a document in my pocket, signed by the state's chief psychiatrist, certifying to my sanity. Now, surely, and even though our mental hospitals are crowded to twice their capacity, he wouldn't have declared me sane if—"

"Okay," she cut in flatly. "Okay. You stays right there, an' I gives you a drink, awright."

She turned away from the screen. I could not see what she was doing, but I heard water gushing into what apparently was a large flat pan.

Hastily, I got off the steps and moved back into the yard. "Listen, listen," I said. "You don't need to do that. I'm leaving right now."

She came to the door again, eyes sparkling in malicious triumph. She said that I had *better* leave, and stay left.

"But you had better not," I said. "Listen, listen, Miss Hattie. Leave the house at no time. Particularly do not leave it at night. Great evil will befall you if you do."

A trace of fear tightened the contours of her off-ivory face. "Huh! What make you think I goin' anywhere?"

"Listen, listen," I said. "Because it is so written that you may, and that great and dreadful evil will result. So it is written. But listen, listen. If I had a drink—a very large one—I could doubtless change the writing."

I had been too eager. She let out a grunt of relief and unbelief, and returned to the kitchen.

I continued on my dreary, drinkless way.

Frequently, or I should say occasionally, I have had some success at the courthouse. There are always a number of loafers around; also, needless to say—and if you will excuse the redundancy—the county office-holders. So I went there today, hoping to amuse them as I sometimes had in the past. To titillate and entertain them with my wisdom, and thus obtain a few coins. Alas, however! Alas, and verily, and lo. Seldom have I been appreciated less than on this day, the day when my need was greatest.

I was chased out of office after office. I was brushed aside, cursed out, elbowed and shoved along by one loafer after another.

. . . I had been unwilling to call on Pete Pavlov, except as a last resort, for a couple of reasons. For one thing, it was quite a long walk across town to the beach area; an almost intolerable walk for one in my condition. For another, I had called upon him so often in the past that further appeals would not only be embarrassing, but were apt to prove fruitless.

There was nothing else to do now, however; and when there is nothing else to do I do what there is nothing else to do.

Shaking and wobbling, I walked the several blocks through town, entered the dance pavilion and crossed the wide, waxed floor to the door of his office. He was bent over an account ledger, cursing and mumbling to himself now and then as he turned its pages. I waited, nervously, my hands twitching and trembling even as the leaves of an aspen.

Not many people will agree with me, but Mr. Pavlov is a very kindly, soft-hearted man. On the other hand—and everyone *will* agree with me on this—he is no fool. And the merest hint, intentional or no, that he might be will send him into an icy rage.

He looked up at last, took the tobacco cud from his mouth, and dropped it into a convenient gaboon. "What the hell you want?" he said, wiping his hand on his pants. "As if I didn't know."

"Listen, listen, Mr. Pavlov," I said. "Humiliated and embarrassed though I am, I find myself impelled to—".

He yanked open a desk drawer, took out a bottle and glass and poured me a drink. I gulped it, and extended the glass. He returned it and the bottle to the drawer.

"Tell you what I'll do with you," he said. "I'll—no, you listen—listen for a change! You go back there in the john and wash up—and use some soap, by God, get me?—and I'll stake you to a square meal."

I said, certainly, certainly, yessir: I could certainly use a good meal. "You can give me the price of the meal now, Mr. Pavlov. That will save time and time is money, and—"

"And the farmer hauled another load away," said Mr. Pavlov. "Just keep on standing there, arguing with me, and you won't get nothing but a kick in the butt."

He meant it; Mr. Pavlov always means what he says. I departed hastily for the washroom. After all, this was the best offer I had had all day—the meal, I mean, not the kick—and I had a notion that it might be improved upon.

I washed thoroughly: my hands, wrists and those portions of my face that were not covered by beard. It was probably as clean as I have been during the thirty years of my existence.

I returned to the office, where Mr. Pavlov complimented me reservedly.

"Looks like you got a few coats of rust off. Why don't you chop that damned hair and them whiskers off, too? Ought to, by God, or else buy yourself a bedsheet and sandals."

"Listen, Mr. Pavlov," I said. "I will do whatever you say. If you would like to give me the money for a barber—or a bedsheet and sandals—along with the price of a meal, I will—"

"I ain't giving you a nickel," said Mr. Pavlov. "I'll take you to a restaurant and pay your check myself."

I protested that he was being unfair: it was implicit in our agreement that I should spend the money on liquor. He grunted, studying me with thoughtfully narrowed eyes.

"Shut up a minute," he said. "Goddammit, if I give you another drink, will you shut up and let me think?"

"Listen, Mr. Pavlov," I said. "For another drink, I would —would—"

I broke off helplessly. What wouldn't one do when he is slowly being crucified?

I snatched the drink from his hand. I took it at a gulp, noting that he had left the bottle on the desk in front of him.

"Huh-uh," he said, as I extended my glass. "Not now, anyways. I got something to say to you, and I want to be damned sure you understand."

"Listen," I said. "I understand much better when I'm drinking. The more I drink the more my understanding increases."

"Shut up!" There was a whip-like crack to his voice. "Now, here's what I was going to say, and you'd better not repeat it, see? Don't ever peep a word about it to anyone. Suppose I was to give you something of mine. Kind of let you take it away from me. I mean, nobody would know that it was you that took it, but— Goddammit, are you listening to me?"

"Certainly, certainly, yessir," I said. "If you were thinking about pouring a drink for yourself, Mr. Pavlov, I will take one, too."

"Dammit, this is important to you," he said. "There'd be a nice piece of change in it for you, and all you'd have to do is—" He broke off with a disgusted grunt. "Hell! I must be going out of my mind to even think about it."

"You appear very depressed, Mr. Pavlov," I said. "Allow me to pour a drink for you."

"Pour one for yourself," he snarled, with unaccustomed naivete. "Then you're gettin' the hell out of here to a restaurant."

It was a quart bottle, and it was practically full.

I picked it up, and ran.

I hated to do it, naturally. It was not only ungrateful, but also shortsighted; in eating the golden egg, figuratively speaking, I was destroying a future hen. I did it because I could not help myself. Because it was another nothing-else-to-do.

When a man is drowning, he snatches at bottles.

I ran, making a wild leap toward the door. And I tripped over the doorsill, the bottle shot from my hands, and it and I crashed resoundingly against the ballroom floor.

I scrambled forward on my stomach, began to lap at one of the precious puddles of liquor.

Mr. Pavlov suddenly kicked me in the tail, sent me scooting across the polished boards. He yanked me to my feet, eyes raging, and jerked me around facing him.

"A fine son-of-a-bitch you turned out to be! Now, get the hell out of here! Get out fast, and take plenty of time about showing up again."

"Certainly," I said. "But listen, listen, Mr. Pavlov. I—"

"Listen, hell! I said to clear out!"

"I will, I am," I said, backing out of his reach. "But please listen, Mr. Pavlov. I will be glad to assist you in a fake holdup. More than glad. You have been very good to me, and I will welcome the opportunity to do something for you."

He had been moving toward me, threateningly. Now he stopped dead in his tracks, his face flushing, eyes wavering away from mine.

"What the hell you talkin' about?" he said, with attempted roughness. "You better not go talkin' that way to anyone else!"

"You know I won't," I said. "I don't blame you for distrusting me after the exhibition I just put on, but—"

He snorted half-heartedly. He said, "You're crazy. Crazy and drunk. You don't know what you're sayin'."

"Yes, sir," I said. "And I don't know what you said. I didn't hear you. I wasn't listening."

I turned and left. I went out onto the boardwalk, wondering if this after all was not the original sin, the one we all suffer for: the failure to attribute to others the motives which we claim for ourselves. The inexcusable failure to do so.

True, I was not very prepossessing, either in appearance or actions. I was not, but neither was he. He was every bit as unreassuring in his way as I was in mine. And as you are in yours. We were both disguised. The materials were different, but they had all come from the same loom. My eccentricity and drunkenness. His roughness, rudeness and outright brutality.

We had to be disguised. Both of us, all of us. Yet obvious as the fact was, he would not see it. He would not look through my guise, as I had looked through his, to the man beneath. He would not look through his own, which would have done practically as well.

It was too bad, and he would be punished for it—as who is not?

And I was in need of more—much, much more—to drink.

Down at the end of the walk, a girl was standing at the rail, looking idly out to sea. I squinted my eyes, shaded them with my hand. After a moment, she turned her head a little, and I recognized her as the vocalist with the band.

She was clad in bathing garb, but a robe was draped over the rail at her side. It seemed reasonable to assume that the robe would have a pocket in it, and that the pocket would have something in it also.

I walked down to where she stood. I harrumphed for her attention and executed a low bow, toppling momentarily to one knee in the process.

"Listen, listen," I said. " 'How beautiful are thy feet with shoes, O, my princess. Thy—' "

I broke off abruptly, noting that her feet were bare. I glanced at her midriff, and began anew:

" 'Thy navel is like—' "

"You get away from me, you nasty thing, you!" she said. "Go on, now! I don't give money to beggars."

"But who else would you give money to?" I said. "Not, surely, to people with money."

"You leave me alone!" Her voice rose. "I'll scream if you don't!"

"Very well," I said, and I moved back up the boardwalk. "Oh, verily, very well. But beware the night, madam. Lo, and a ho-ho-ho, beware the night."

The warning seemed justified. Molded as she was, the night could hold quite as much danger for her as it did delight.

Ahead of me, I saw Mr. Pavlov come out of the pavilion and swagger away toward town. Studying him, his high-held head, the proud set of his shoulders, the hurt I had felt over his caution in talking to me was suddenly no more.

He had behaved thusly I knew—I *knew*—because he actually did not intend to perpetrate a fake holdup. He neither intended to nor would. He might think the contrary, go so far as to plan the deed. But he would never actually go through with it.

He was as incapable of dishonesty, of anything but absolute uprightness, as I was of sobriety.

He turned and entered the post-office building. I crossed to the other side of the street, continued on for another block and suddenly lurched, and remained lurched, against a corner lamppost.

People passed by, grinning and laughing at me. I closed my eyes, and murmured alternate threats and pleadings to the Lord World.

Halfway down the block, there was a grocery store. Mr. Kossmeyer, the lawyer who comes here every summer, was parked in front of it, loading some groceries into the back seat of his car.

I pushed myself away from the lamppost, and stepped down into the gutter. I walked down to where Mr. Kossmeyer was, and tapped him on the shoulder.

He jumped, cursed and banged his head. Then, he turned around and saw that it was I.

"Oh, hello, Ganny," he said. "I mean—uh—Judas."

"Oh, that's all right, Mr. Kossmeyer," I laughed. "I know I'm not really Judas. That was just a crazy notion I had."

"Well, that's fine. Glad you've snapped out of it," Mr. Kossmeyer said.

"I'm really Noah," I said. "That's who I really am, Mr. Kossmeyer."

"I see," he said. "Well, you shouldn't have to travel very far to round up your animals."

He sounded rather wary. Disinterested. His hand moved toward the front door of his car.

"Listen, Mr. Kossmeyer," I said. "Listen. I'm accepting contributions for an ark, materials or their monetary equivalent. Planks are a dollar each, Mr. Kossmeyer."

"They ain't the only thing," said Mr. Kossmeyer. "So is a quart of wine."

He seemed a lot smarter than he used to be. Summer a year ago, I sold him a reservation to the Last Supper.

"Listen, Mr. Kossmeyer, listen," I said. "All the world's a stage, and all the actors, audience; and the wise man casteth no stink bombs. Doesn't that stir you, Mr. Kossmeyer?" I said.

"Only to a limited degree," said Mr. Kossmeyer. "Only to a limited degree, Noah. I feel nothing at all in the area of my hip pocket."

"Listen, Mr. Kossmeyer, listen," I said. "They've got a new resident out in The City of Wonderful People. They've got a man that's TRULY HUMBLE. He's TRULY HUMBLE, but he always acted like the snootiest, most stuck-up man in town. You know why he acted that way? You know why, Mr. Kossmeyer? Because he was so lonesome for

company. The planks are really only ninety-eight cents, Mr.
Kossmeyer, and I can bring back the change from a dollar."

"A little more finesse," said Mr. Kossmeyer. "A little
more english on the cue ball."

"Listen," I said. "Listen, Mr. Kossmeyer. I'm thinking
about digging him up, and putting him on television. There
ought to be millions in it, don't you think so? A TRULY
HUMBLE man, just think of it, Mr. Kossmeyer!"

"I think I'll drive you down to the library," said Mr.
Kossmeyer, "and lead you to the history section."

"I could put falsies on him, Mr. Kossmeyer," I said. "I
could teach him to sing and dance. I could—listen, Mr.
Kossmeyer, listen, listen. There's a couple of other new resi-
dents out in The City of Wonderful People. They're
MOTHER AND FATHER, and they're the most wonderful
of all. Listen, Mr. Kossmeyer, listen. They're DUTIFUL
AND LOVING PARENTS, they're GODFEARING AND
LOYAL, they're HONEST and KINDLY and STEADFAST
and GENEROUS and MERCIFUL and TOLERANT and
WISE and—"

"What the hell they got, for God's sake?" said Mr. Kossmeyer. "A tombstone or a billboard?"

"Listen, Mr. Kossmeyer," I said. "Listen. It's the teensiest
stone you ever saw. Not much bigger than a cigarette package. I figure that fellow who writes on the heads of pins
must have done the inscription. It's practically impossible to
read it, Mr. Kossmeyer. Virtually impossible. They've got
all those virtues, yet no one can see them. You know why
it's that way? You know why, Mr. Kossmeyer? Listen, listen, listen. It's supposed to be symbolic. It's symbolic, Mr.
Kossmeyer, and I just remembered you can get a pretty good
grade of plank for—"

"Listen, Noah, listen, listen," said Mr. Kossmeyer.
"Which is the shortest way to that building-supply store?"

VII

Hattie

I GUESS I just don't think no more. Not no real thinking, only little old keyhole kind.

Reckon you know what I mean. Reckon you know what it does to a body. May be a mighty big room, but you sure ain't going to see much of it. And you keep looking through that keyhole long enough, nothing ain't never going to look big to you.

Get to where that eye of yours just won't spread out.

Used to think pretty tolerable, way back when, long long time ago. Back when Mr. Doctor was talking to me and teaching me, and telling me stuff. Seemed like I was just thinking all the time, and thinking more all the time. Big thinking. Almost could feel my brain getting bigger. Then, we comes here and that was the end of that and the beginning of the other.

Mr. Doctor stopped; stopped himself from pushing me on, and stopped me from pushing. Just wouldn't do, he said. Got to be in a certain place, so I got to fit in that place. Don't do nothing that would maybe look like I don't belong in that place. Just sink down in it, and don't never raise my head above it.

Too bad and he sure hates it, Mr. Doctor said. But that's the way it's got to be. And what good's it going to do me, he said, filling my head full of a lot of stuff I wasn't never going to use?

Guess he right, all right. Anyways, he stop with me. Me, I didn't put up no fuss about it. Catch me arguing with Mr. Doctor. Never did it but the once, long long time ago, and maybe that used all my arguing up. Took all my fighting for the one battle, maybe. And maybe I just didn't see no call to fight.

Don't work up no sweat going down hill. Awful easy thing to do, and that little old keyhole at the bottom, it don't bother you at all.

Can't think no more. Ain't got the words for it. Mr. Doctor, he tell me one time back when he was telling me things, he tell me the mind can't go no farther than a person's 'cabulary. You got to have the words or you can't talk, and you got to have 'em or you can't think. No words, no thinking. Just kind of feeling.

Me, I get hungry. I get cold and hot. I get scared, and sick. Mostly, I get scared and sick. Scared-sick, kind of together. And not doing no real thinking about it. Just feeling it and wishing it wasn't, and knowing it's going to go right on being. A lot worse maybe.

Because he, that boy, he acting nice now. He trying to pretend being friendly. And that boy, he act that way, you sure better watch out for him. He sure about to get you then.

He come out in the kitchen other night after supper. Right there with me before I know it. And he smile and sweet-talk, and say he going to help me with the dishes.

"Go 'way," I said. "You lea' me alone, hear?"

"Well, we'll let the dishes go," he said. "Let's go in your bedroom, mother. I have something I want to talk to you about."

"Huh-uh. No, suh," I said. "You ain't gettin' me in no bedroom."

"I'm sure you don't mean that," he said. "You're my mother. Every mother is interested in her son's problems."

I go in the bedroom with him. Scared not to. He got his mind made up, and that boy make up his mind, you sure better not get in his way.

Meanest boy in the world, that boy. Just plain lowdown rattlesnake mean.

I get on bed. Get way back against the wall with my legs drawn up under me. He sit down on chair at side of bed. He takes out a cigarette, and then he looks at me, and asks if it's all right he could smoke.

I don't say nothing. Just keep my eyes on him, just watching and waiting.

"Oh, excuse me, mother," he said. "Allow me."

He stick a cigarette at me. He strike a match and hold it out, and me I put that cigarette in my mouth and puff it lit. Had to. Scared to death if I don't, and scared if I do.

I take a puff or two, so's he won't go for me. Then, he start talking, ain't watching me close, I squeeze it down in my fingers and let it go out.

"Now, it's a money problem I wanted to discuss with you, mother," he said. "Largely one of money. I don't suppose you have a considerable sum you might lend me?"

"Huh," I said. "Where I get any money?"

"I'd probably need several thousand dollars," he said. "There'd be some traveling to do. I need enough to get reestablished, for two people to live on, for an extended period."

"Why'n't you go away?" I said. "How I get any money, I don't draw no wages? You want money you knows who to go to."

He look at me a little while. He look right on through my head it seem like, and I figure he's really about to come after me. Figure I really make one big mistake in kind of talking back to him. But what else I do, anyhow? Can't be nothing much but back-talk when you talk to him.

Can't think no more.

Can't do nothing, and can't do something.

Scared if I do and scared if I don't.

He go on looking at me, and I know my time really come. Then, he say, that's perfectly all right, mother. Say he really didn't expect me to have any money, but he thought he should ask. Say it might've hurt my feelings, him needing money and not giving his mother the 'tunity to help.

Crazy-mean, that boy. He nice and polite that way, he crazy-meaner than ever.

"But you're quite right, mother," he said. "I do know where to get it. Or, more accurately, I know where I could lay my hands on a large amount of money. The difficulty is that there is another person who needs it—who will need it, I should say. His situation is quite similar to my own, and it would place him in a position practically as difficult as mine if he didn't have it. So under the circumstances—what do you think I should do, mother?"

"Huh?" I said. "What? What you talkin' about, boy?"

"I'm sorry," he said. "Please don't feel I don't trust you, mother; it isn't that at all. It's just that you might be placed in a very compromising situation if I gave you any details, spoke in anything but the most general terms. And I believe you can advise me quite as well on that basis. What's your best opinion, mother? If you were in my place, would you feel justified in extricating yourself from an untenable position at this other man's expense?"

What I think? Me—what *I* think? What I got to think with? Or listen with, or talk with?

That mean boy, I see him too well'n too close—plenty too close, a mean-crazy boy like him—but I sure don't hear him. Might as well be talking a zillion miles away.

"Lea' me alone," I said. "Why you all the time devilin' me? I ain't done nothin' to you."

"Relatively," he nodded. "Yes, I see. Relatively, you have done nothing. And, of course, you meant that as an answer to my question. You did mean it so, didn't you, mother?"

"Fo' God's sake," I said. "Fo' God's sake, jus'—"

"I suppose it's always that way, don't you, mother? It's inevitable. There are certain rigid requirements for being one's self, a tenable self. They may not be violated, despite any exigencies, regardless of the temptation and the nominal ease with which violations could be accomplished. Otherwise, he becomes another. And how, if he can't cope with the problems of his own self—live in pride and contentment within its framework—can he dwell in that other? Obviously, he can't. He loses identity. He may have been little, but now he is nothing. He doesn't know what he is. Yes, you're absolutely right, mother. I'm so glad you could advise me out of the background of your experience."

Don't know what he talking about.

Don't want to know.

"Now, there's another thing I wanted to ask you about, mother," he said. "Since I can't help myself—am past the point of help, let's say—should I help this other man? Should I remove an obstacle in the path to the solution of his problem? I have nothing to lose. It would help him immensely. In fact, he might not be able to bring himself to do it. Or if he did, he might suffer from regrets. It might cast a pall over the goal he achieves by so doing. How do you feel about it, mother? Do you think I should help him or not?"

How do I feel? What he care? What do I think? Think nothing. Just think nothing.

Can't.

Him, he might be talkin' about killing someone, and I wouldn't know it.

He look at me, one of them pretty-smooth eyebrows cocked up, them even pretty-white teeth showing; kind of smiling and kind of frowning. And I know he as mean-crazy as they come—you just look at that boy and you see he is. But for maybe a second or two I don't see it. What I see is sort of a picture that all at once just popped up out of nowhere, that kinda seemed to wooze out of my eyes and spread itself over him. And me—I—I almost laugh out loud.

I think—thought, *"Why, my heavens, Hattie, what in the world has come over you? How can you be afraid of this fine young man, your son? What . . . ?"*

The picture go away, back wherever crazy place it come

from. Me, she, the me that'd thought them words go back to the same place. Nothing but the regular me, now, and it don't do no thinking. Don't see nothing but through that bitty old keyhole. Just sees meanest boy that ever lived.

He been that way for years. I watch it coming on him. Oh, sure, he don't do nothing with it for a long time. He wait until he big and strong. But I see it all right, he *let* you see it. He nice and polite all the time, but he let you see it; make you know what you can 'spect. Poke it right at you.

"Yes, mother?" he said. "Can you answer my question?"

"Go 'way?" I said. "How I know? I—me—"

"Why, of course," he said. "Naturally, you wouldn't know. It's not something a person can advise another about, is it? The individual concerned has to make his own decision. Thank you, very much, mother. I can't tell you what a comfort it's been to talk over my problems with you. Now, I see you're looking a little tired, so perhaps I'd better..."

He stand up. He put one knee on the bed, and start to lean over toward me. Smiling that pretty white-teeth smile, fastening on to me with them soft brown eyes. An'...

Knew I was going to get it then. He had been playing around, all politey and smiley, and now he going to do it. Something mean. Something bad. Had to be, because there couldn't be no other be. Couldn't think of no other. Couldn't think no more but little old keyhole stuff.

Don't know what I going to do. House almost in a block by itself, and I yell my lungs out and no one hear me. No good yelling. Couldn't do it nohow, scaredysick as I was. Couldn't do nothing nohow. Just ain't nothing to do but wait, and hope he won't be too mean. No meaner than I can stand.

Can't move. Feel like I frozen, I that stiff and cold. Can't hardly see nothing. Just kind of a white blur moving toward me, pushing right against my face. Then, I can't really see nothing. Just feel something, sort of soft and warm, pressing me on the forehead.

It go away. I get my eyes open somehow, and he standing back on the floor again.

"Good-night, mother," he said. "I hope you sleep well, and please don't worry about anything. After all, there's no longer anything to worry about, is there?"

He stand there and smile, and I figure he really going to get me now. He just been playing around so far, but now he through. Can't scare me no worse, so now he going to get me.

He turn around and leave. He close the door real gentle-like. But, me, I ain't being fooled. Ain't going to get me out there where he probably hiding, all set and waiting for me. Just about bound to be.

Why he act like he do if he ain't up to something? Why he make all that talk to me? Why he keep calling me mother and be so nicey-nice, and—an' kiss me goodnight?

Huh! Me, I know that boy. Seen that meanness coming on him a long, long time. He up to something all right. Fixing to get me.

I hear front door open. Hear it close.

I hear his car starting up, going away.

And all at once, I just flop over on my face and cry. Because he *ain't* got me, and he *ain't* going to. Him or nobody else.

Can't.

Just ain't nothing to get.

VIII

Luane Devore

IT WAS MONDAY night. The dance pavilion is closed for business that night, but of course Ralph still has things to do there. Or things to do somewhere.

It was a little after eight, a little after dark. I heard the front door open quietly.

I hadn't heard Ralph's car, but I naturally assumed it was Ralph. The house is well-insulated. If he had driven up the old lane from the rear—as he sometimes does—I wouldn't have heard the car.

I turned around slightly in the bed. I waited a second, listening, and then I called, "Ralph?"

There wasn't any answer. I called again, and there still wasn't any. I made myself smile, forced a laugh into my voice.

Ralph is such a tease, you know. He's always playing funny little jokes, doing things to make you laugh. I suppose he seems pretty dull and stodgy to most people, but he's really worlds of fun. And it's always that sweet, silly puppyish kind. Even while you're laughing, you get a lump in your throat and you want to take him in your arms and pet him.

Oh, I can understand his attraction for women. His looks and youthfulness are only part of it. Mostly, it's because you enjoy being around him. Because he's so funny and sweet and simple and . . .

"Ralph!" I called. "You answer me now, you bad, bad boy. Luane will be terribly angry with you, if you don't."

He didn't answer. He—whoever it was—didn't. But I heard the floor creak. I heard more creaks, coming nearer, moving slowly up the stairs.

Just the creaks, sounds; not footsteps. Nothing I could identify.

I called one more time. Then, I swung my feet out of bed and . . . and sat there motionless. Half paralyzed with fear, helpless even if I was not so badly frightened.

The phone was out of order. *As he—this person—doubtless knew.* It was useless to yell. And if I locked the door, well, it could be forced. And then I would be trapped in here, in this one crowded, cluttered room, with even less chance of saving myself than I had now.

I got up, took an uncertain step toward the door. I hesitated, stared slowly around the room. And suddenly I was almost calm.

Save myself! I thought. Save myself!

Now, surely I should know how to do that.

Kossy came to see me the first Sunday of the season. I had called him, indicating that there was something I wanted to talk to him about when he had the time—strictly at his own convenience. And he raced right over. He didn't hurry on my account, of course. Catch one of *those* people doing anything for you unless there's a dollar in it. Probably he thought Ralph would be here, and he could load up on a lot of free eggs and fruit and vegetables.

Oh, well. I suppose I am exaggerating a little. Kossy really doesn't seem to care about money; he'll treat you just about the same way, whether he's getting a fat fee or nothing. And I suppose my call may have sounded rather urgent. But—

But why should he care about money? I wouldn't either if I had all he's got. Why should he blame me, a poor, helpless sick old woman for sounding a little excited?

He was very mean and insulting. Not that he usually isn't. As soon as I was convinced that there was nothing to worry about, I ordered him out of the house. I should have done it long before, because I'd heard some pretty unpleasant stories about that man. How he'd cheated and swindled people right out of their eyeteeth. I can't say just who I heard them from, but they're all over town. And where there's so much smoke, there must be some fire.

At any rate, he not only insulted me, but he gave me some very bad advice. Because I most certainly did have something to worry about! He convinced me temporarily—and against my will—that I hadn't. But I knew better. The season was only two days old, and I'd already seen it in Ralph —seen it in the way he talked and acted and looked. And that was only the beginning.

He came home late that night, very late, I should say, since he is always out working as long as he can find work to do. I sleep a lot during the day, however, so I was awake.

He fixed a snack for me; he was too tired to eat, himself, he said. He was going to go straight to bed—in fact, he got a little stubborn about it. But I cried a little and pointed out how lonesome it was for me all day by myself, so we talked a while.

I studied him, listening to what he said, noticing what he didn't. I began to worry again. I began to get frightened.

I hardly slept a wink all night. I hardly slept a wink any night, because Ralph didn't change back to what he had been—he kept going farther and farther the other way.

I was practically out of my mind by the end of the week. I was going to call Kossy, but I didn't have to. He came to see me. As of course, I should have known he would. Catch *him* letting go of a good thing! He's probably building up his bill, so that he can attach this property.

Anyway, he was afraid not to come. He knew what I could do if I took the notion. I've never said anything about him yet, mind you—hardly anything—but if he wanted to be mean and ugly, I certainly had a right to defend myself!

I cried a little, and told him about Ralph. He sat and stared at me like I was some strange kind of animal, instead of a poor, sick, helpless old woman who needed comfort and sympathy. And then he said that he'd be goddamned.

"Kossy, darling," I said. "I've asked you so many times please not to use—"

"I tell you what I won't use," he said. "I won't use any words you ain't used ten thousand times yourself. I hadn't ought to bother with you at all, but as long as I am I'll—"

"All right, Kossy, dear," I said. "I'm just an old woman. I can't stop you if you insist."

"Luane," he said. "For God's sake— Aaah, nuts—" he said, and threw up his hands. "Never mind. Let me see if I got this straight. Ralph is seeing this girl every night; you're sure of that. But he *isn't* sleeping with her. And you're bothered because he *isn't!*"

I said, no, Ralph wasn't. "He always has before," I said. "He's a-always been honest before—c-come home and told me about it afterwards."

"But—but—" He waved his hands again. "You mean you want it that way? You want him to make these babes?"

"W-well. I don't really want him to," I said. "But it wouldn't be fair to stop him, since I—well, you know. And as long as he tells me about it . . ."

He gave me an odd look, as if he was a little sick at his stomach. He said something about, yes, he could see how I might enjoy that.

"Well, never mind," he went on. "It kind of knocked me over for a minute, but I guess I get the picture. Ralph is playing it clean with this gal. In your book, that makes him in love with her. Suppose he does a switch, goes after what he always has, what does that make him?"

"Please," I said. "Please don't joke about it, Kossy."

"Okay," he shrugged. "Say he's in love with her. Say he's

going to stay in love. And you don't like it, naturally. But it don't add up to his planning to kill you."

"But it does! I mean, it could," I said. "I—well—"

"Yeah?" He waited, frowning at me. "How does it? I seem to remember that we were all over that the other day. Ralph could get a divorce. He could just up and leave. We agreed that he could."

"Well," I said. "I guess he could—I mean, I know he could. But—but—"

"Yeah?"

He stared at me. He—and that shows what a crook he is! Honest people move their eyes around. They don't have a guilty conscience, so they don't feel they have to brazen someone down. It's only crooks who do that.

"Okay," he said. "You want to hold out something, go ahead. It ain't my neck."

"But I'm not," I said. "I—it's just that when I talked to you the other day, I didn't know he was so serious about this girl. I—"

"So now you know. And he can still walk away or get a divorce, so it still don't shape up to a murder."

"I—well, here's what I was thinking," I said. "The season will end in a couple months, and of course the girl will be leaving. So whatever . . . if Ralph is going to do anything, he'll have to do it by then. And—and—"

Kossy waited a moment. Then he grimaced and reached for his hat.

"Don't!" I said. "I'm trying to tell you, Kossy. After all, it isn't easy for me to discuss Ralph this way, to think of some reason why my own husband would w-want t-to—to—"

"Well, sure." He cleared his throat uncomfortably. "I don't suppose it is. But—"

"But there is a reason why he might, Kossy. This property isn't worth nearly what it used to be, but it would still bring five or six thousand dollars—maybe as much as ten. And if Ralph needed money, if he was so mean and selfish that he couldn't wait until I died . . ."

Kossy's eyes narrowed. Blinked. He nodded slowly.

"Yeah," he said. "Could be. That would seem like a world of dough to Ralph, particularly now that he's been so hard hit in the job department. I don't suppose there's any use pointing out to you that if Ralph is planning something, you're at least partly at fault."

"I am not!" I said. "I haven't said a single solitary word about anyone! Anyway, Ralph doesn't blame me in the least, he knows I haven't said half as much as I could have, and—"

"Okay. Okay," Kossy sighed. "Forget it. Ralph wants to kill you, maybe. He's got a double motive, maybe: to clear his way for the girl, and to cash in on what's left of the estate. Say that that's the situation. What do you want me to do about it?"

"Well, I . . ."

I didn't know. How should I know what to do? That was his job. And he'd been plenty well paid for it! I hadn't ever actually caught him stealing from me, but there'd been a great deal of talk about—

"You think it over," he said. "See what develops, and we'll talk again in a few days. Meanwhile, I want to say something about these lies of yours—*shut up! don't interrupt me!*—and I want you to take it to heart. If—"

"But I haven't said a word!" I said. "Honestly, Kossy. I— And I just hope someone does try to start something! I'll—"

"You'll damned probably get killed," he said. "I mean it, Luane. It's the law of averages. You get enough people sore enough to kill you—and you've got just about the whole damned town—one of them is almost certain to do the job. So cut it out, get me? Better still, see if you can't undo some of the damage. Try to do it. Admit you've been lying, apologize to the people you've harmed. Use that phone for something decent for a change."

Well, of course, I wasn't going to do anything like that! I'd die before—I just wasn't going to do it! In the first place, I hadn't said anything. He was just irritated by the few harmless little jokes I'd told about him. In the second place, it was all true what I'd said; and I guessed that if anyone was cowardly enough to harm someone for telling the truth, they'd have done so by now. And just what was I supposed to do all day, pray tell? Just lie here all day like a bump on a log, and never have a little harmless chat with anyone?

I tried to explain to Kossy how absolutely ridiculous it all was. But just try to tell *that* man anything! He looked at me, not really listening to what I was saying, and then he sighed and shook his head.

"Okay, maybe you can't help it," he said. "Take it easy, and I'll see you in a few days."

I was just a little worried after he'd gone; I mean, about someone wanting to kill me besides Ralph. Then, I just shoved it out of my mind—almost—because a person can only worry about so much and that's all, and I had more than my limit with Ralph.

Because I hadn't told Kossy everything. I hadn't told him the most important thing.

He came back the latter part of that week. He kept coming back, week after week—he was here the last time this morning—but it didn't help any. I certainly couldn't do any of the silly things he suggested.

Ralph hadn't said or done anything out of the way. He was different, but it wasn't something you could put your finger on. Outwardly he was just as nice and considerate as ever, so how could I have put him under peace bond? Obviously, I couldn't. I wouldn't have even if I had a concrete reason to, because that *would* have fixed things up. It would have brought everything to a showdown—killed the last bit of hope I had. And the same thing would happen if I let Kossy speak to him. Or if I had one of the county authorities do it.

Ralph wouldn't feel sorry for me any more. He wouldn't pity me. He'd just go ahead and do what he wanted to do— what he wasn't yet nerved-up to doing.

As you can see, Kossy has been absolutely no help to me. None whatsoever. Here I am, a sick old woman whom nobody loves, and I can get no help from my own attorney, a man who has stolen thousands of dollars from me.

The foolish little squirt even brought a gun here, a revolver, and wanted me to keep it! I refused even to touch it.

"Oh, no, you don't!" I said. "No, siree! People have accidents with guns. Accidentally-on-purpose accidents. As soon as Ralph or anyone found out I had that thing, they'd fix up a little accident for me."

"But, dammit, Luane," he said. "What the hell else can you do? What can I do for you? Now, you keep it—keep it where you can get to it fast. And if anyone goes for you, use it."

"*Wh-aat?*" I said. "You're suggesting that I should *shoot* someone? W-why—why, how dare you, Kossy! What kind of woman do you think I am?"

"God!" he almost shouted. "I don't know why the hell I don't kill you myself!"

He said some other very mean, nasty things, and then he slammed out of the house.

He came back for the last time this morning.

He said that he still thought I was in much more danger from others than I was from Ralph. Then, when I said he simply didn't know what he was talking about, he began to get ugly. And nosy.

"Y'know, Luane," he said, "the more I think about it, the less I can see Ralph committing murder for the few thousand bucks this estate would bring. It's hard for me to see him as a murderer, anyway, and for that kind of dough it just don't seem to figure at all."

"Well, you're absolutely wrong," I said. "For a man like Ralph, who's never really had anything—"

"Uh-huh. Because he's cautious, ultra-conservative. Ralph wouldn't bet that the sun comes up in the east unless he got a thousand-to-one odds! He'd take no chance except for something big. He—no, now, wait a minute! Let's take a good look at Ralph. He's been odd-jobbing around this town for more than twenty years. Working around people who are hip-deep in dough—who are almost disappointed if they don't get chiseled. But did Ralph ever clip one of 'em? Did he ever pad a bill, or walk off with a few tools or steal gasoline and oil, or pull any of the stunts that a guy in his place ordinarily would? Huh-uh. Never. In all those years, he—"

"Oh, yes, he did!" I said. "He most certainly did! How do you think he got that car, pray tell?"

"Not by killing anyone. Not by running any real risk at all. In all those years, he pulls just one perfectly safe bit of chiseling—and he collects a high-priced car!" Kossy shook his head slowly, giving me that mean, narrow-eyed grin. "Who are you kidding, sister? You know goddamned well Ralph wouldn't kill you for this estate. If you really thought he would, you'd just sign it over to him."

"Why, I would not!" I said. "There'd be nothing to stop him then. It would be just like throwing him in that girl's arms!"

"Well?" he shrugged. "What choice you got? What choice has Ralph got? How you going to get by if he stays here?"

"Why, we'll get by just fine!" I said. "We'll—uh—"

"Yeah? How will you? Out with it, goddammit!"

"Well, we'll— You leave me alone!" I said. "You stop it! You're j-just as mean and hateful as—as—" And I broke down and began to cry. Undignified as it was, and as much as I despise weepy women.

That's probably how that girl holds on to Ralph—by crying all over him. Making him feel sorry for her. Ralph is so good-hearted, you know. He hates to see anyone unhappy, and he just won't let them be. And they just about can't be when he's around. He's so much fun, so sweet and funny at the same time, and—

At least, he was—the mean, selfish thing! Why, even this morning, he was carrying on pretty much as he used to. And it was just pretense, of course, but I almost forgot that it was, and . . . and it was nice.

"Come on, Luane," Kossy said. "Let's have it."

"I c-can't!" I said. "I don't know what you're talking about. You leave me alone, you mean hateful thing, you!"

"Look, Luane—" He put his hand on my shoulder, and I shook it off. "Don't you see it, honey? Don't you see that you can't hold Ralph in a trap without being in it yourself? Of course you do. That's why you're so frightened, as you have every right to be. Let him go, Luane. Let him out of that corner you've got him in. If you don't . . ."

"K-Kossy," I said. "Kossy, d-darling . . . you don't really think he would, do you? Y-you said you didn't—couldn't see him k-killing—"

"God!" He slapped his forehead. "Oh, God! I— Look. Tell me what it is, what you're squeezing Ralph with. I have to know, don't you understand that?"

"I k-know . . . I mean, I *can't!*" I said. "There isn't anything, and—don't you dare say there is! Don't you dare tell anyone there's something—that I'm—"

He sighed and stood up. He said something about my being his client, God help him, whatever that meant: probably that it wouldn't be ethical for him to say anything. Not that that would stop him, of course. He's always talking, saying mean things about me. I haven't said anything half as mean about him as he has about me. Every time he leaves here, he goes around laughing and telling people how old and ugly I look.

Anyway, he certainly doesn't know anything. He's always contradicting himself, saying one thing one minute and something else the next.

First he tells me that Ralph won't kill me, and then he says he will. He says that Ralph won't, but that there's plenty of others who might. And if *that* doesn't prove he's crazy, what would? Kill me—a bunch of cowardly, lying, lowdown sneaks like they are! They don't have the nerve. They have no reason to. I've never done anything to harm them.

I've never harmed anyone, Ralph least of all, but now . . . *NOW!*

. . . Ralph? Is it Ralph on the stairs?

But why won't he answer me? What can he gain by not

answering? Why is he doing it—if it is he, if he is going to—this way?

To lure me out there? Maybe I shouldn't go. But if I don't . . .

It must be someone else. It simply wouldn't make sense for Ralph to do it this way. As for someone else, why would they—he—she . . . ?

They're afraid, unsure? They haven't made up their mind? They're waiting to see what I do? They're trying to lure me out of the room—like Ralph would, is, might?

If I only knew, I might save myself. If I knew who it was—before the person becomes sure—I might save myself.

If . . . If I go out. If I don't go out.

Save me, I prayed. Just let me save myself. That's all I want. It's all I've ever wanted. And that's certainly not very much to ask, is it?

I went out.

I saw who it was.

IX

Danny Lee

ALTHOUGH I AM but of a humble station in life, I come from a proud old southern family, which was directly descended from that proud old southern warrior, Robert E. Lee, and we lived in a proud southern village which shall here be Nameless. Then, when I was but a slip of a girl, I loved unwisely and not too well, and my proud old father drove me out into the storm one bitter night. So, I went to a large city where I stumbled anew into a new pitfall. I mean, I didn't do anything wrong, really. Never again did I repeat my first and only fatal mistake. But there was this place I worked in where you could hustle drinks and where if you could sing a little or dance or something like that, you could keep whatever the customers gave you. And one night an orchestra leader entered its portals, and I innocently agreed to accompany him to his room. I didn't have the slightest idea of what evil designs he wanted. I simply went because I felt sorry for him, and I had to send some money back to my invalid mother and my two brothers, and—

Oh, I did not! I'm making all of this up.

I don't have any mother or brothers or any family except my father, and if he has anything to be proud of I don't know what it is. The last time I heard he was in jail again for bootlegging back in our home town.

He had a little two-by-four restaurant. I used to serve drinks to the customers, and two or three times when it was someone I liked real well and I simply had to have something to wear or go naked, I let them you-know. I finally picked up a dose from one of them. Pa said that as long as I got it, I could figure out how to get rid of it. So I stole ten dollars he had hidden, and went to a place near Fort Worth.

I couldn't get a restaurant job, which was the only kind of work I knew, since I couldn't get a health certificate. And I couldn't get that, of course, until I got over the dose. So practically flat broke as I was—without even money enough for a room—it looked like I was really in a pickle.

I said it *looked* that way. Because actually, I guess, it was lucky I didn't have room money. Otherwise, I wouldn't have gone into that cheap little burlesque house just to rest a while and try to think.

There were four chorus girls in the line. Pretty old girls, it looked like. I didn't think they could sing half as good as I could, and the dancing they did was mostly just wiggling and shaking. I watched and listened to them a while. Finally, I got up enough nerve to go to the manager and ask him for a job.

He took me into his office. I sang and wiggled for him, and he said I was okay, but he didn't have a job open right then. Then, he winked and asked me how about it—you know—and said there was a fast ten bucks in it for me. I told him I couldn't. He offered me twenty, and I told him no again. And I told him why, because it would be a dirty trick on him. He was awfully appreciative. He said most girls in my position would have taken the money, and not given a damn whether they dosed some poor son-of-a-bitch. (Those are his own words and I'm only repeating them because I want to tell the whole truth and not leave out anything. Not a bit more than I have to. I don't use that kind of language myself.)

He appreciated my telling him so much that he gave me a job after all. He had to fire another girl to do it, and naturally I was sorry for that. But she was really too old to be working, anyway. I told her so, when she started cursing me out. And she didn't have much to say after that.

I started seeing a doctor right away—as soon as I got a paycheck. He got me cleared up fast and things were pretty nice from then on. For quite a while. All the men who came to the show—you hardly ever saw a woman—liked me. They'd start clapping and whistling and calling for me, even while the other girls were doing their numbers. Then, when I went on stage they wouldn't let me go. They were really crazy about me, even if it doesn't sound nice for me to say so, and I couldn't begin to tell you how many of them tried to date me up. If I'd been willing to you-know for money like some of the other girls did, I could have made all kinds. I wouldn't have had to just barely skimp by like I was doing, because that manager could really squeeze a quarter until the eagle screamed. But, anyway, I didn't do it. Not even once, as much as I was tempted.

I remember one time when I just about had to have a new pair of shoes, and I saw an absolutely darling pair in a window, marked down from twenty-three ninety-nine to fourteen ninety-eight. It was such a wonderful bargain, I just didn't see how I could pass it up. I felt like I'd die if I didn't have those shoes! And while I was standing there a man who came to the show all the time came along, and offered to buy them for me. But I turned him down. I hesitated a moment first, but I did.

My real name is Agnes Tuttle, but I changed it when I went to work at the show. I was going to make it something kind of unusual, like Dolores du Bois. But the other girls had given themselves fancy names—Fanchon Rose, and Charlotte Montclair and so on—so I decided to make mine simple. It seemed best to, you know. It stood out more. And if I'd had the same sort of name as those other girls, people might have thought I was cheap and shoddy, too.

I'd been at the show about six months when the police raided it and closed it down. The manager got a big fine, and had to leave town. The girls went back to doing what they had been doing, which was you know what. I hardly knew what to do.

I felt it would be kind of a step down to take a waitress job. There's nothing wrong with being a waitress, of course. But it doesn't pay much, and it's darned hard work. And in view of my experience, I felt that I simply ought to and had to have something better. I was like that then; awfully ambitious, I mean. Willing to do almost anything to be a big-name singer or something like that. Now, I feel just about the opposite. In the first place, I know I'm not much good as a singer and never will be, like Rags McGuire says. In the second place, I just don't care. All I want now is just to be with Ralph, forever and always—and by golly, I *will* be!—and . . .

But I'll tell you about that later.

I didn't have money to travel on, and there weren't any jobs like I wanted in Fort Worth. Oh, there were a few, of course, but I couldn't get them. All the talent for them was hired through New York agencies, so I didn't stand a chance, even if I'd had the training and the presence and the clothes. I guess I was pretty awful, then. And I don't just mean my voice. I tried to wear nice things without being flashy, and I tried to be careful about makeup and using good English. But trying isn't enough when you don't have money to work with, and you're not sure of what you're trying for.

I guess I couldn't really blame Rags for thinking I was something that I wasn't.

I was working in a beer garden at the time I met him. It wasn't a very nice place, and it wasn't a real job. I just hung out there, like several other girls did. I got to keep any money a customer gave me for drinking with him, and I also got a commission on what he bought. Then, a few times a night I'd sing a number. And the orchestra and I divided the change that the customers tossed up on the bandstand.

Well, Rags dropped into the place one night, and a waitress tipped me off that he was a big spender. So, after I'd done a number, I went over to his table. I didn't know who he was—just about the greatest jazz musician of all time. I just thought, you know, that if he was going to throw money around, he might as well throw some my way. And I thought he looked awfully interesting too.

Well. I guess I did just about everything wrong that I could. I just botched everything up, not only that night but the next day when he gave me a singing try-out, and offered me a contract. I—I just don't know! I still squirm inside when I think about it. But I know I didn't act that way just because of the money. I wanted to get ahead, of course, but mostly I wanted to please him. I thought I was doing what he wanted me to do, and he seemed so terribly unhappy I felt that I should. But . . .

He had no use for me from then on. From then on, I was just dirt to him. He wouldn't let me explain or try to straighten things out. I was just dirt, and he was going to keep it that way.

I tried to excuse him. I told myself that if I'd had a family like his, and the same terrible thing happened to mine that happened to his—though he won't admit it did—why, I might be pretty hard to get along with, too. But, well, you can't keep excusing people forever. If they're simply determined to despise you, you just have to let them. And all you can do about it is to despise them back.

Rags has just done one nice thing for me in all the months I've worked for him. That was when we came here, and he introduced me to Ralph. He didn't mean to be nice, of course. He meant it as a mean joke on me—telling me that Ralph was a very wealthy man and so on. But that was one time Mr. Rags got fooled. Ralph told me the truth about himself that very first night, and I told him the truth about myself. And instead of being mad and disappointed with each other, like Rags thought we would, we fell in love.

Ralph was so cute when he told me about himself. Just like a darling little boy. All the time he was talking I could hardly keep from taking him in my arms and squeezing him. He couldn't make a living any more in this town, it seemed, because everyone was mad at his wife. On the other hand, he'd lived here all his life, and he wouldn't know what to do anywhere else. Not by himself, I mean. And the idea he kind of had in mind in meeting me was—well, he got pretty mixed up at that point. But I understood him, the poor darling. He didn't need to put it into words for me to understand, any more than he's had to put certain other things into words.

While he was hesitating, not knowing quite how to go on, I patted him on the hand and told him to never mind. I said I was awfully glad he seemed to think so much of me because I liked him a lot, too. But maybe if he knew the truth, he'd change his opinion of me.

Well, he didn't try to shut me up like most men would have. You know, just say to forget it and that it didn't matter. He just nodded kind of grave and fatherly-like, and said, "Is that a fact? Well, maybe you better tell me about it, then."

I told him. Everything there was to tell, although I may possibly have forgotten a few little things. When I finally stopped, he waited a minute, and then he told me to go on.

"G-go on?" I said. "But that's all there is."

"But I thought you were supposed to have done something bad," he said. "Something that might change my mind about you."

Well . . .

My eyes misted over. I could feel my face puckering up like some big old baby's. I sat there, looking and feeling that way and not knowing what to do. And Ralph reached out and pulled my head against his chest.

"You go right ahead, honey," he said. "You just cry all you want to."

Well, I cried and I cried and I cried. It just seemed like I could never stop, and Ralph told me not to try. So I cried and I cried. And everything that was in me that wasn't really me—that didn't really belong there—was kind of washed away. And I felt all clean and nice and peaceful. And I was never as happy in my life.

Ralph . . .

I know I get pretty silly whenever I start talking about him, but I just can't help it. And I just don't care. Because however much I rave, I still don't do him justice. He's the handsomest thing you ever saw in your life, for one thing. A lot handsomer than most anyone in pictures—and don't think I won't make him try out for pictures when we get away from here! But that's only one thing. Along with it, he's just the nicest, kindest, understandingest—well, everything. He's mature, and yet he's awfully boyish. The most wonderful sweetheart a girl ever had, but kind of fatherly, too.

We saw each other every night after that. We talked about what we were going to do—kind of talking around the subject. Because it looked like there was just about only one thing we could do. And things like that, they're not something you can very well talk about.

Yes, that mean old hen he was married to would give him a divorce, all right. Or he could just leave, like I'd suggested, and to hell with the divorce. She'd let him know that—those things—although she hadn't said so in so many words. The trouble was she wouldn't let him take the money that belonged to him, money he'd worked for and saved dollar by dollar. She wouldn't even let him take half of it. She kept it under the mattress of her bed, and she made it clear to him that anyone who got it would have to kill her first.

Ralph was afraid to sue her. He had a record book of his savings, showing when and how much he put away. But that wouldn't necessarily prove that the money was his, would it? She might have told him to keep the record for her. And, anyway, those lawsuits drag on forever, and the only ones that get anything out of 'em are the lawyers.

At first, I told Ralph to let her keep the money, the old

bag! But Ralph didn't want to do that; we'd need it ourselves to get a decent start in life. And after I thought about it a while, I wouldn't have let him if he had wanted to.

It was his money, wasn't it? His and mine. When something belongs to a person, they ought to have it and if someone tries to stop them *they* ought to have something.

I told Ralph that he ought to speak up to her, instead of just beating around the bush. I said that I'd be glad to talk to her myself, and if that didn't do any good I'd slap some sense into her. But Ralph didn't think that would be a very good idea. And I guess it wasn't.

She'd probably put the money in the bank, and tell the police she'd been threatened. Then, if anything happened, why you know where we'd be.

I was sorry afterwards that I'd said anything like that to Ralph. Because I was perfectly willing to do what I said I would and heck of a lot more. But it might have sounded a little shocking to say so. I mean, even if I wasn't a woman, if I was Ralph, say, and I said something like that to me, why I'd—oh, well, you know what I mean.

It was best to keep things the way they'd been, except for that once. Talking about what had to be done, but not *really* talking about it. Not actually admitting that we were talking about it.

By doing that, you see, we'd never really know. There'd never be anything to make us uncomfortable about each other. After all, she was a pretty old woman. Her health was bad, and everyone in town hated her guts. And, well, all sorts of things could happen to her, without us having a thing to do with them.

And neither of us would need to know that we had unless . . .

The weeks raced by. They went by like days, and before we knew it the season was almost over. And we were still talking, and nothing had happened.

Then, that Monday night came.

The dance hall was closed that night. Ralph was working there—not any regular hours, but just until he got through.

We weren't seeing each other afterwards, because I had a sore throat.

I don't know how I got it exactly. Maybe from sleeping in a draft. Anyway, it wasn't really bad, and if I'd been anything but a singer I wouldn't have bothered to call a doctor.

I was sitting out on the stoop when he came. He painted my throat, looking kind of nervous and haggard, and then he asked me why I hadn't been in the first time he called.

"I spend thirty minutes finding the right cottage," he said, "and then when I finally locate it—"

"I'm so sorry about that, doctor," I said. "You see, I was taking a shower, and it was some time before I heard you calling and pounding at the cottage next door. I came right out as soon as I did, but—"

"W-what?" he said. "The cottage next . . . ?"

"Uh-huh. It's unoccupied; so many of them are . . . But I thought you saw me, doctor. I ran out on the stoop and called to you, just as you were driving away, and I thought you called and motioned to me. I supposed you meant you had no more time right then, and you'd have to come back later."

He looked at me blankly for a moment. Then, his eyes flickered in a kind of funny way, and he snapped his fingers.

"Why, of course," he said. "Now, that I see you in the light, I can . . . You had a robe on, didn't you, and a—uh —did you have a bathing cap?"

"That's right," I said. "A robe and a bathing cap, because I'd just come out of the shower. I suppose I looked quite a bit different than—"

"Not a bit," he said firmly. "Not a particle. I'd have recognized you instantly, if it hadn't been so fixed in my mind that you were in the other cottage. Let's see, now—about what time was that?"

I told him I guessed it was a little after eight. Somewhere along in there. Just about the time it was getting dark.

"You're right," he said. "You're absolutely right, Miss Lee. Let me compliment you on your memory."

"Now, that's real sweet of you, doctor," I said. "But, after all, why shouldn't I remember? I mean, a girl just about *couldn't* forget anything connected with a distinguished-looking gentleman like you."

I smiled at him, looking up from under the lids of my eyes. He beamed and harrumphed his throat, and said I was a very fine young lady.

He repeated that several times while he was repacking his medicine kit. He said he wanted me to take very good care of myself, and any time I needed him, regardless of the hour, I was to let him know.

I thought he was awfully sweet and nice. Kind of distinguished and mature, like Ralph. He asked if he might use my phone, and I said, why certainly, and he called a number.

"Hank?" he said. "Jim . . . Just wanted to tell you that it's—you know—all right . . . I remembered where—I mean, I can account positively for the time. There's a young lady who saw me, recognized my car and my voice, and . . . Who? Well, that one. The one we were discussing. She— What? Why—yes, I suppose that's true. I hadn't thought about it that way, but . . ."

I'd gone over by the door to be polite; so that it wouldn't look like I was snooping, you know. He turned around and looked at me, kind of frowning as he went on talking.

"Yes. Yes, I see. Naturally, unless I was sure that she— unless there was an observer I could hardly be observed. But . . . Yes, Hank. That's the way I feel. On the one hand . . . Absolutely. Had to be. No reason to consider it anything else . . . Exactly, Hank! And as long as that's the case . . . Fine, ha ha, fine. See you, Hank . . ."

He hung up the receiver. He picked up his medicine kit, gave me a funny little nod, and started out the door. On the stoop he paused for a moment and turned around, facing me.

"Allow me to compliment you again," he said. "You're a very smart young woman, Miss Lee."

"Now, that is *sweet*," I said. "That's a *real* compliment . . . coming from a smart man like you."

I gave him another under-the-eyelids smile. He turned suddenly, and left.

I thought he seemed a little cranky. I wondered if he thought I hadn't really seen him that first time—because actually, I hadn't. I said I had because he'd started off being so cross, and I was afraid he might think I hadn't been at home when he called. But all I'd really seen was his car driving away. Or a car that looked like his.

Oh, well. Probably I was just imagining things. After all, he remembered seeing me perfectly, so why should he think I hadn't seen him?

I put on some make-up and went out on the beach. I sat down with my back to the ocean. After a while, I saw a light come on in Rags McGuire's cottage. I walked down to it, and knocked on the door.

He was sitting on the side of the bed, drinking out of a bottle. He's been drinking a lot lately, but on Mondays he drinks more than usual.

"Well!" he said. "If it isn't little Miss Bosoms, the girl with the tinplated tonsils! How come they let you out, baby, or ain't you been in yet?"

"I don't know what you're talking about and I don't care," I said, "and all I've got to say to you is I'm quitting, you mean, hateful, dirty old—old—"

"Bastard, son-of-a-bitch, whoremonger," he said. "Now, you sit right down there, honey, and I'll think up some more for you. I'll do that, an' you tell me where you were around eight o'clock tonight."

"If it's any of your business," I said, "I was in my cottage at eight o'clock and for all the rest of the evening. I had a sore throat, and the doctor saw me about eight and again just a little while ago, if it's any possible concern of yours."

His eyes widened. He broke out laughing suddenly, slapping his knee. "Doc Ashton? Oh, brother! You two—you *and* Doc Ashton! Will this burn a certain little lawyer I know! Who dreamed it up, baby, you or Doc?"

"I haven't the faintest notion of what you're talking about," I said. "But since you seem to be so curious as to my whereabout at certain times, perhaps I might inquire about yours."

His laugh went away. He put the bottle on the floor, sat staring into the neck of it as if there was something there besides the whiskey.

"I don't know," he said. "I don't know where I was. But I was all alone, Danny. I was all alone."

It seemed awful silent then. The only sound was the waves, lap-lapping, whispering against the sand.

I began to get sort of a funny feeling in my throat. I was just about to say I'd work out the rest of the season—these last two weeks—but he spoke first.

"So you're quitting, huh? Well, that's something. That's at least one break you've given me."

Then he got up and came over to me, and took my face between his hands. "You didn't mean it, Danny, and I didn't mean it. Besides, I don't want you to leave, Danny. Besides, I love you, Danny."

He stooped and kissed me on the forehead.

I said, "Rags . . . Oh, g-gosh, Rags. I—"

"I couldn't keep you any longer," he said. "I couldn't pay you, understand? But I think you're one of the finest girls I've ever known, and I think you have one of the very finest voices I've ever heard. I wished you'd go on with it; I did wish that. But now . . . now, I know you mustn't. It would never do. Because the one thing is all you can have, Danny —the music is all you can have, Danny—and if it isn't enough . . ."

He took his hands away from my face, let them slide down my arms. Then he scowled suddenly, and gave me a shake. "Posture!" he said. "Goddammit, how many times do I have to tell you? You've got two feet, haven't you? You're not an obstetrical case, are you? Well, stand on them then, by God."

I said I was sorry. I stood like he'd told me to, like he'd taught me to.

"All right," he said. "Let's have it. Make it *Stardust*.

Even you can't bitch that one . . . Well, what are you waiting for?"

"I—I c-can't!" I said. "Oh, R-Rags, I—"

He ran his hands through his hair. "Okay, go on! Get the hell—no, wait a minute. Sit down over there, right there, dammit. I'll let you hear *Stardust* like it ought to be sung . . . almost."

I sat down by his desk. He sat down in the other chair, and put in a long-distance call to his wife.

The call went through, and he held the receiver a little away from his ear.

"Hi, Janie," he said. "How's it going? How are the boys . . . ?"

I couldn't understand what she said, because it was just kind of sounds instead of words. A sort of quack-quacking like a duck would make.

"They're asleep, eh? Well, that's fine. Don't bother to wake them up . . ."

The boys couldn't be waked up. Never, ever.

"Listen, Janie. I've got a kid here I want you to sing for. I—*Janie!* I said I wanted you to sing, understand? . . . Well, get with it, then. Give me *Stardust* and give it loud. This kid here is pretty tone-deaf . . ."

She couldn't sing, of course. How can you sing when you don't have a nose and only part of a tongue, and no teeth . . . and hardly any place to put teeth? But there was a click and a scratch; and her voice came over the wire.

It was pretty wonderful, her singing *Stardust*. A platter has to be pretty wonderful to sell three million copies. But Rags had started frowning. He squirmed in his chair, and the cigarette in the corner of his mouth began a kind of nervous up-and-down moving.

He held the receiver away from him. He looked at it, frowning, and then he lowered it slowly toward the hook. And the farther down it went, the farther it was away from him, the more his frown faded. And when it was completely down, when the connection was broken, he wasn't frowning any more. He was smiling.

It was a kind of smile I'd never seen before. A dreamy, far-off smile. One of his hands moved slowly back and forth, up and down, and one of his feet tap-tapped silently against the floor.

"Do you hear it, Danny?" he said softly. "Do you hear the music?"

"Yes," I said. "Yes, I hear the music, Rags."

"The music," he said. "The music never goes away, Danny. The music never goes away..."

X

Henry Clay Williams

I KNEW FROM the moment I sat down at the table that morning that I was in for trouble. I knew it before Lily had said a word. Probably most men wouldn't have, even if they had lived in the same house with a sister as long as I have with Lily, but I'm an unusually close observer. I notice little things. No matter how small it is, I'll see it and interpret it. And nine times out of ten my interpretation will be correct. I've trained myself to do it. A man has to, as I see it, if he wants to get ahead. Of course, if he doesn't, if he wants to remain a small-town lawyer all his life instead of becoming the chief legal officer of the sixteenth-largest county in the state, why that's his privilege.

I began to eat, knowing that Lily was going to land on me, and why, and trying to prepare myself for it. Finally, when she still held back, I gave her a little prod.

"I notice you're running low on pepper," I said. "Remind me to bring some home tonight."

"What? Pepper?" she said. "What makes you think I'm running low?"

"Why, I just supposed you were," I said. "You have plenty? There's still plenty in your kitchen shaker?"

She sighed, and pursed her lips together. She sat looking at me silently, her glasses twinkling and flashing in the morning sunlight.

"I just wondered," I said. "I noticed that you only peppered one of my eggs when you cooked them, so . . ."

"Is there a pepper-shaker in front of you?" she said. "Well, is there or isn't there, or hadn't you noticed?"

She sounded unusually irritable for some reason. I said, why, of course, I'd noticed the shaker, and it didn't matter at all about the eggs.

"I was simply curious about them," I said. "You always pepper them, each one the same amount, so naturally I wondered why you hadn't—"

"I see," she said. "Yes, I can see how you might get pretty excited about it. It would be a pretty big thing to a big man like you."

"Now, I didn't say I was excited," I said. "I said nothing of the kind, Lily. If my memory serves me correctly—and I think you'll agree that it usually does—the words I used were 'curious' and 'wonder.'"

I nodded to her, and put a bite of egg in my mouth. Her lips tightened, then she spoke shaky-voiced. "So you were curious, were you? You were wondering? You were curious and wondering about why I hadn't peppered an egg! Well, I'll tell you something I'm curious and wondering about, and that's what you intend to do when you are no longer the chief legal officer of the sixteenth-largest county in the state. For after the elections this fall, Mr. Henry Clay Williams, *you're going to be out of a job!*"

She deliberately timed that last with the moment when I was taking a swallow of coffee to wash the egg down. I coughed and choked, feeling my face turn red. The egg tried to go one way and the coffee another, and for a long moment I was certain I'd strangle.

"Now, goddammit," I said, when I was able to speak. "Why—what the hell—"

"Henry! *Henry!* Don't you use that language in this house!" Lily said.

"But—it's—it's crazy! Outrageous! Why, I've always been—I mean I've been county attorney since—"

"Very well," she said. "Very well, Henry. But don't forget that I warned you."

She got up and started to clear off the table. I hadn't finished breakfast yet—although I certainly didn't feel like eating any more—but she went right ahead, regardless.

The bulge under her apron seemed larger today. I glanced quickly away from it, as her eyes shifted toward me. It was very annoying, that tumor. Having to live with it constantly, and yet never daring to look at it, let alone to discuss it. Perhaps it wouldn't have been for most men, but when you have trained yourself as I have—when you are used to observing and . . .

I observed that her glasses had an unusually high sparkle this morning. Obviously, then—I was immediately aware—there must be some dust on them. She couldn't keep her glasses clean, and yet she was trying to pass herself off as a prophet!

I was about to make some pointed reference to these facts. But she left for the kitchen at that moment with a load of dishes, and when she returned I decided it wasn't wise. After all, you don't cure a trouble by adding to it. That's always been my policy, at least, and it's worked out very well. If—

Out of a job! Lose the election!

She was seated at the table again. She looked at me, nodded slowly, as if I had spoken out loud.

"Yes, Henry. Yes. And if you had any brains at all, you wouldn't need me to tell you so."

"Now, see here, Lily," I said. "I—"

"Any brains at all, Henry. Or if you were even capable of listening. Hearing anything besides the sound of your own voice or your own thoughts, anything that might deflate the largest ego in the sixteenth-largest county in the state. You're a fool, Henry. You're a—"

"I am, am I?" I said. "Well, I guess I know how to keep my glasses clean, anyway!"

The glasses flickered and flashed. Her eyes squeezed shut behind them for a moment. Then, she opened them again, keeping them narrowed; and her nostrils twitched and flared. And I knew the explosion was coming.

"Listen to me, Henry. What I'm saying is not for myself. I don't expect *you* to have any consideration for me, your own sister who has practically given up her life for you, taken care of you since you were wet behind the ears. I don't expect you to care if I'm so slandered and gossiped about that I'm almost ashamed to go out in public. I'm only concerned about you, as I've always been, and that's why I'm saying you are going to lose the election unless you get up a little spunk, and act like a man for a change instead of a fat, blind, stupid, egotistical *jellyfish!*"

She paused, breathing heavily, her bosom heaving up and down. I was going to say something back to her, but I decided it wasn't worthwhile. I couldn't lose the election. I—why, I just *couldn't*. And when a person can't do something . . .

"Yes," she said. "Yes, you can, Henry. You know I'm right. You know you don't have good sense. You—shut up when I'm speaking to you, Henry! *Henry!*"

"I'm not saying anything," I said. "All I was going to say was—"

"Nothing that would make any sense, that's what you were going to say. You were going to say that no one in this town pays any attention to Luane Devore, but they do, all right. Perhaps they don't believe what she says, but they remember it—and they wonder about it—and when a man is a spineless incompetent to begin with, it doesn't take a deal of wondering to dump him out of his sinecure. At any rate, you seem to have forgotten that it takes more than the town vote to elect you. You have to have the farm people, and they don't know that when Luane Devore says you—we—that she's lying!"

"Well, they will," I said. "After all, you've had that tumor quite a while now, and when you don't have a—I mean, when nothing happens, why—"

I swallowed back the words. I looked down at my plate, tried to keep my eyes there, but something seemed to pull them back up.

She stared at me, silently. She sat there, staring and waiting. Waiting. Waiting. Waiting and waiting.

I threw my napkin on the table, and jumped up.

I marched to the telephone, and asked for the Devore residence. There was a lot of clicking and clattering; then the operator said that the Devore line was out of order.

"Out of order, eh?" I said. "Well—"

Lily took the phone out of my hands. She said, "Did you say the Devore line was out of order, operator? Thank you, very much."

She hung up and put the phone back on its stand. It seemed to me that she owed me an apology for doubting my word, but naturally I didn't get one. Instead she asked me what I was going to do about the line being out of order.

"Why, I'm going to fix it, of course!" I said. "I'm a telephone repair man, ain't I?"

"Please—" She put her fingers to her forehead. "Please spare me your attempts at humor, Henry."

"Well, I'll wait until it's in order. Naturally," I said. "I'll call her later on from the office."

"But suppose it isn't repaired today?" She shook her head. "I think it would be best to go and see her, Henry. Lay down the law to her in person. Tell her that if she doesn't stop her lies, and if she doesn't issue a public retraction immediately, you'll have her indicted for criminal slander."

"But—but, look," I said. "I can't do that. I mean, going out and jumping all over a sick old woman, and—and it wouldn't look right! No matter what she's done, why, she's a woman, a sick old woman, and I'm a man—"

"Are you?" Lily said. "Then, why don't you act like one?"

"Anyway, it's—it's probably illegal," I said. "Might get into a lot of trouble. I'm a public official. If I use my public office in a personal matter, why— All right!" I said. "Go ahead and shake your head! You're doggone good at telling someone else what to do, but when it comes to doing it yourself that's something else again, ain't it?"

"Very well, Henry." She turned away from me. "Could I impose on you to the extent of driving me out there?"

"Why, certainly," I said. "I'm always gl—*what?*"

"I'll see her myself. I'll guarantee that by the time I'm through, she'll have told her last lie. And if you don't want to drive me out, I'll walk. I'll—"

Suddenly, she was crying, weeping wildly. Suddenly, all the coldness and calmness were gone, and she was a different woman.

It was like that time years ago, when we were kids out on the farm. She'd taken me down in the meadow that day to search out some hens' nests. We came to one, half-filled with eggs, and just as she reached for it, a rattlesnake reared up on the opposite side. And what happened then—my God!

She busted out bawling, but it wasn't the usual kind. Not the way people cry when they're frightened or hurt or something like that. It was, well, wild—crazy. More like real mean cussing than bawling. It scared hell out of me, a six-year-old kid, and I guess it did the same to the snake, because he tried to whip away. But she wouldn't let him. She grabbed up that deadly rattler in her bare hands, and yanked him in two! Then she threw the pieces down, and began to jump on them. Bawling in that wild, crazy way. And she didn't stop until there wasn't enough left of that snake to make a grease spot.

I've never forgotten how she acted that day. I don't think I ever will. If I'd had any idea that my harmless little remark at breakfast would have started anything like this . . .

"I'll take care of her! I'll fix that filthy slut! I'll t-teach her how t-to—"

"Lily!" I said. "Listen to me, Lily! I'm going to—"

"You! You don't c-care! You don't know what it means to a woman t-to— I'LL CLAW HER EYES OUT! I'LL PULL

*HER FILTHY TONGUE OUT OF HER THROAT! I'LL—
LET GO OF ME! Y-YOU LET—"*

I didn't let go. I held on tight, shaking her as hard as I
could. And I didn't like doing it, you know, but I was more
afraid not to.

As soon as she was quieted enough to listen, I began to
talk. To tell her and keep telling her that I'd see Luane Devore myself. That I definitely and positively promised I
would. I kept repeating it until it finally sank in on her, and
she snapped out of her fit.

"All r-right, Henry." She shuddered and blew her nose. "I
certainly hope I can depend on you. If I thought for a moment that—"

"I told you I would," I said. "I'll do it this evening. Right
after I close the office."

"After? But why can't you—?"

"Because," I said, "it's a personal matter; you can't get
around that. Even seeing her after office hours could put me
in a pretty awkward position if someone chose to make anything out of it. But I certainly can't do it on the county's
time."

She hesitated, studying me. At last, she sighed and turned
away again.

"All right," she said. "But if you don't really intend to, I
wish you'd say so. In fact, the more I think about it, the less
I care whether you do talk to her. I'm perfectly willing to do
it myself—I'd *like* doing it—"

"I said I'd do it," I said. "Immediately after five tonight.
Now, it's all settled, so forget it."

I left before she could say anything more. I drove down to
the courthouse, and went up to my office.

It was a pretty busy morning, all in all. I had a long talk
with Judge Shively about the coming election. Then, Sheriff
Jameson dropped in with a legal matter, and I had another
long conference with him. As you may or may not know, a
sheriff gets part of his income from feeding prisoners. This
county pays Jameson fifty cents per meal fed, and what he

wanted to know was, could he feed them one double meal a day instead of two, and still collect a dollar.

Well, it was a pretty fine legal point, you know. Something you might say was this way or that, and you could make a case out either way. I finally decided, however, that there might be just a leetle danger in the double-meal proposition. But I pointed out that the word meal could mean just about whatever he wanted to. A bowl of beans could be a meal or a plate of fried potatoes, or even a hunk of bread.

It was eleven o'clock before I got Jameson straightened out. I was hoping I'd have time to take a deep breath— maybe get out and see a few voters—but it just wasn't in the cards. Because now that I'd gotten all those other things cleared up, why, Nellie Otis, my secretary, needed me.

Oh, I didn't really mind. Nellie is an attractive young woman, as well as an excellent secretary and there are twelve votes in the Otis family—and she's always so appreciative of everything I do for her.

She stood by watching, all the time I was untangling the ribbon on her typewriter. She said she just didn't know how I did it; she'd tried and tried herself, and she'd just made it worse. I said there was nothing to it, really. It was just a matter of going straight to the *source* of the trouble, like it would be in any other problem.

I passed it off lightly that way, but it *was* a pretty bad snarl. Just about the worst I'd ever untangled for her, and that's really saying something. By the time I'd finished with it, and gotten washed up, it was five minutes after twelve. The whole morning was gone, and I was already into my lunch hour.

I was turning away from the washroom sink when I happened to glance out the window. And I just stood there for a moment, staring, wondering well, what the hell next.

Now, there, I thought, that's really something. Kossmeyer and Goofy Gannder! One great man talking to another great man. Yes, sir, I thought, water really finds its level.

Mind you, I have nothing against Kossmeyer. I've never said a word against him to anyone. But I do feel—yes, and

I'm justified—that if he's what's supposed to be smart, why, I don't want to be.

The way I look at it, if he's so damned smart, why isn't he rich? Where's the proof that he's smart? Why, half the time he don't even use good English!

I had him figured right from the beginning. He's one of those jury jaybirds, one of those howlers and pleaders. All the law he knows you could put in your right eye. And he's just been lucky, so far. If he ever came up against a man who dealt in *facts* and *details*, I guess you know how long he would last.

I went to lunch.

The afternoon was even busier than the morning.

The way the work was piling up, it began to look like I might be so tied up I couldn't get out to see Luane Devore tonight. But, then, I thought about the way sis had acted, and I decided I'd better, work or no work.

I was on my way out of the courthouse when Sheriff Jameson called to me and asked me to step into his office. He'd confiscated a batch of evidence, and he wanted my opinion of it before he went into court on it. I tested it. I told him I wouldn't hesitate to go before the Supreme Court with evidence like that. So he laughed, and gave me a bottle to take with me.

It was a little after five when I got in my car and headed out of town. Just before I got to the Devore place, I took a right fork in the road and drove up toward the hills. The land up there isn't much good any more. Either worn out, or eroded and gullied of its topsoil. All the farms have been abandoned, including the one where I was born and raised.

I turned into the lane that led up to our house. I stopped in the yard, all grown up to weeds now, and looked around. One side of the barn-loft was caved in. All the windows of the house were broken, and the kitchen door creaked back and forth on one hinge. And the chimneys had toppled, scattering brick across the rotting and broken shingles of the roof.

It was kind of sad. Somehow it made me think of that

poem, *The Deserted Village*, I used to give at Friday afternoon school recitals. It was sad—but it was nice. Because everything had gone to hell now, but in my mind it hadn't. In my mind, nothing had changed; everything was as it used to be. And the way it used to be . . . nothing was ever nicer or finer than that.

No worries. No one fussing at you. Always knowing just what to do and what not to do, and knowing that it would be all right if you made a mistake. Not like it is now, when you mean well but you ain't real sure of yourself, and there's no one to come straight out and set you straight.

Not like it is now, when people can't understand that you're truly sorry about something—and being sorry is about all you can do—and they wouldn't give a damn if they did understand.

I took a big drink of the whiskey. I guessed I ought to be seeing Luane Devore, but it was so nice and peaceful here, and I had all evening to do it. So I got out, and went up the back walk to the kitchen.

The big old range was still there. Lily had said what was the sense of moving an old wood-burner into town, for pity sake. So we'd left it behind, and consequently, fine stove that it was, it was rusting into junk. It looked like junk. But in my mind I could see it like it had been. Like I'd used to keep it when I was a kid, and Mama and Papa were still alive.

That was my job, keeping the stove blacked and polished. I did it every Saturday morning, as soon as it was cooled off from breakfast, and no one was allowed in the kitchen while I was doing it. First, I'd take a wire brush and dry-scrub it all over. Then, I'd get busy with the blacking rags and polish. I'd rub it in good, get it wiped so clean you couldn't raise a smudge on your finger. After that, I'd take a little kindling splinter and tip it with the blacking, and get down in all the little cracks and curleycues.

We didn't do any farm work on Saturdays, except for just the milking and feeding, of course. So when I was through,

I'd roll back the doors to the living room, and Mama and Papa and Lily would come in.

Mama would take a look, and kind of throw up her hands. She'd say, why, I just can't believe my eyes; if I didn't know better I'd think it was a new stove! And Papa would shake his head and say, I couldn't fool him, it *was* a new stove. I'd gone out and snuck one in from somewhere, and no one could tell him different. So, well, I'd have to take and show him that it was really just the same old stove, and . . .

Lily hardly ever said anything.

I used to wonder about it, wanting to ask her why but somehow kind of shy about doing it. And one time when I'd saved up a lot of nickels—I got a nickel every time I polished the stove—I took them all and bought her a big red hair-ribbon. I brought it home from town inside my blouse, not telling anyone about it. That night, when she was out in the kitchen alone doing dishes, I gave it to her. She looked at it, and then she looked at me smiling at her. Then she doused it down in the dishwater, and threw it into the slop pail. I watched it sink down under the scummy surface, and I didn't know quite what to do. What to say. I didn't feel much like smiling any more, but I was kind of afraid to stop. I was kind of, well, just afraid. Mama and Papa always said if you were nice to others, why, they would be nice to you. But I'd done the nicest thing I knew how, I thought. So all I could think of was that Mama and Papa must be wrong, or maybe I didn't know what was nice and what wasn't. What was bad and what was good. And for a minute I felt all scared and bewildered and lost. Well, though, Lily grabbed me up in her arms suddenly, and hugged me and kissed me. She said she'd just been joking, and she was just mixed-up and absent-minded and not thinking what she was doing. So . . . everything turned out all right.

I never said anything to Mama or Papa about it. I even lied to Mama and said I'd lost all my nickels when she asked me what had happened to them. That was about the only time I can ever remember her scolding me, or Papa saying anything real sharp to me—because she felt he had to be told about it. But I still didn't tell about the ribbon. I knew they'd be terribly upset and sad if they knew what Lily had done, and I'd've cut off my tongue before I told them. It's funny how—

Dammit, it's not funny! There's nothing funny about it. And why the hell does it have to be that way?

Why is it when you feel so much one way, you have to act just the opposite? So much the opposite?

Why can't people leave you alone, why can't you leave them alone, why can't you just all live together and be the way you are? Knowing that it's all right with the others however you are, because however they are is all right with you.

I wandered through the house, drinking and thinking. Feeling happy and sad. I went up the stairs, and into my little room under the eaves. Dusk was coming on, filling the room with shadows. I could see things like they had been, almost without closing my eyes. It all came back to me . . .

The checked calico curtains at the windows. The circular rag rug. The bookcase made out of a fruitbox. The high, quilted bed. The picture above it—a picture of a boy and his mother, titled *His Best Girl*. The little rocking chair . . .

The chair was still there. Lily hadn't mentioned moving it, and I kind of didn't like to. I hesitated, and then I tried to sit down in it.

I was a lot too big for it, of course, because San—because Mama and Papa had given it to me the Christmas I was seven. I kept squeezing and pushing, though, and finally the arms cracked and split off, and I went down on the seat. That was pretty small for me too, but I could sit on it all right. I could even rock a little if I was careful. So I sat there, rocking back and forth, my knees almost touching my chin. And for a while I was back to the days that had been, and I was what I had been in those days.

Then some rats scurried across the attic, and I started and sighed and stood up. I stood staring blankly out the window, wondering what the hell I'd better do.

Dammit all, what was I going to say to Luane? She'd just start screaming and crying the minute I opened my mouth, and I'd wind up making a fool of myself like Lily says I always do. It wouldn't do any good to ask her for a retraction, because I wouldn't be able to make myself heard in the first place and in the second place she'd know there wasn't a damned thing I could do. She'd know I wouldn't take her into court. Trials cost money, and voters don't want money spent unless it has to be. And they sure wouldn't see it as having to be in this case. They might be sore at her. They might want her to catch it in the neck. But using county money to do it just wouldn't go down with them. Besides that—besides, dammit, I *couldn't* bring her to trial. I didn't dare do it.

She was Kossmeyer's client. He'd fight for her to the last ditch, regardless of what he thought of her personally. He'd fight—one of the best trial lawyers in the country would be fighting *me*—he'd put me on the witness stand and mimic me and get everyone to laughing, and shoot questions faster than I could think. And—

I took a drink. I took a couple more right behind it. My shoulders sort of braced up, and I thought, well, who the hell is Kossmeyer, anyway? He ain't so goddamned much.

I took another drink, and another one. I let out a belch.

He—Kossmeyer—he didn't really know anything. He was just a fast talker. More of an actor, a clown, than he was a lawyer. No good outside of a courtroom where he couldn't pull any of his tricks.

Outside of a courtroom, where he had to deal strictly in *facts,* he'd be no good at all. I could make a fool out of him—with the right kind of facts. It would be all over the county, all over the state, how Hank Williams had shown Kossmeyer what was what.

Maybe . . .

Oh, hell. I just couldn't talk to Luane. She wouldn't listen to me, and—damn her, she ought to be made to! To listen or else. And what, by God, could she do about it if she was? What could Kossmeyer do about it? You'd have your facts all ready, you know. So you'd just smile very sweetly, and say, why, there must be some mistake. The poor woman must have gone *completely* out of her mind. Why, I've been right here at home with my sister all evening. And Lily would swear that I had been, and—

God Almighty! What was I thinking about? I couldn't do anything like—like *that!* I wouldn't any more think of—of —hurting anyone than I would of flying. So . . .

But they kept hurting me, didn't they? They wouldn't leave me alone, would they?

And if I didn't do something, what would I tell Lily?

Could I get away with lying to her again? If I could— give her a real good story and make it sound convincing— why, that would give me some time, and maybe I could think of something to do. Or maybe I wouldn't have to do anything at all. You know how it is. Lots of times if you can put something off long enough, it just kind of takes care of itself.

But I sure hated to try lying to Lily. Remembering the way she acted this morning, it almost made me shiver to think about lying to her.

And why should I have to, anyway? Why not do the other as long as it was perfectly safe?

God, I didn't know what to do! I knew what I ought and wanted to do, but actually doing it was something else.

I looked at the whiskey bottle. It was only a third full. I lifted it to my mouth, and started gulping. I took three long gulps, stopped a second for breath, and took three more gulps. I coughed, swayed a little on my feet, and let the bottle drop from my fingers.

It was empty. My eyelids fluttered and popped open, and I shuddered all over. Then, my shoulders reared way back, and I seemed to have a ramrod where my spine had been.

I gave the bottle a hard kick. I laughed and made a pass in the air with my fist.

I went down the stairs, and drove away.

It was about a quarter of nine when I got home. Lily met me in the hall—all ready, it looked like, to open up on me, so I opened up first.

"Now, just one minute, please!" I said. "You listen for a change, and then if you've got any questions you can ask 'em. Now, you'll recall that—"

"H-Henry. Henry!" she said. "I—I'm—"

"You'll recall—" I raised my voice. "You'll recall that I was against seeing Luane. I told you it was highly inadvisable, occupying the position that I do, but you insisted. So—"

"H-Henry..." she said shakily. "You—you did see her?"

"Naturally. Where do you think I've been all evening?" I said. "Now, it didn't turn out at all well—much worse even than I expected. So whatever you do, don't let on to anyone that I— What's the matter with you?"

She took a step back from me. Her hand fluttered to her mouth.

"Y-you've been drinking," she said. "You d-don't—didn't know what you were—"

"I've had a drink," I said. "Just a swallow or two, and I don't want to hear anything about it. I—"

"Shut up!" Her voice cracked out suddenly like a whip. "Listen to me, Henry! The sheriff called here a few minutes ago. I was positive you were up to something foolish, staying away like this, so I didn't tell him you weren't here. I said you were taking a bath, and you'd have to call him back. Now—"

"B-but why?" My stomach was sinking; it was oozing right down into my shoes. "W-what d-does—"

"You know why, what! Going out there so drunk you—you— You killed her, understand! Luane's dead!"

Doctor Jim Ashton arrived at the Devore place right behind me, and we went in the house together. Jim looked pretty drawn, sickish. Surprisingly—or maybe it wasn't surprising—I'd never felt better or more self-confident in my life. I'd been kind of set back on my heels for a second, but I snapped right out of it. The fogginess washed out of my mind, taking all of the old foggy unsureness with it. I had a keyed-up, coiled-tight feeling, and yet I was perfectly at ease.

Sheriff Jameson and a couple of his deputies were inside. I talked to Jameson, and then I went into the living room and talked to Ralph Devore. He appeared a little stunned, but not greatly upset. He answered all my questions promptly and lucidly. And—I should add—most satisfactorily. I clapped him on the back, offered him my condolences and told him not to worry about a thing. Then, I went back out into the hall.

Luane Devore lay at the foot of the stairs in her night-gown. Although she was sprawled on her stomach, her legs back up on the steps, her head was twisted completely around so that her face was turned upward. Her lips were bruised and swollen, smeared with drying blood. There were several other bad bruises on her face and, of course, her neck was broken.

Jim finished his examination, and we stepped into the dining room to confer. I told him about Ralph, why Ralph had to be completely above my suspicion. He was pretty startled, naturally—I had been myself when I saw the proof of Ralph's innocence. But, then, he shrugged and nodded.

"I'd call it an accident myself," he said. "That's a long fall from the top of those stairs. A fall like that could easily have bruised her up much more than she is. Of course, when someone has lived in hot water all her life, you hardly expect her to die of chilblains, but . . ."

I laughed. I said it was odd that an accident should get her when so many people had motives for doing so. But there it was, wasn't it? He said it was an accident. I said it was. So did the sheriff. That made it an accident, and anyone would have a hell of a time proving that it wasn't.

I laughed again. He gave me an odd, searching look. I hesitated—my laugh had sounded pretty loud, I guess—and then I asked him what was on his mind.

"Well—uh—nothing." He frowned uncomfortably. "You were . . . the sheriff reached you at home tonight?"

"Why, yes," I said. "What of it?"

"Nothing. Lily was there with you, I suppose? Well—" He shook his head. "That's good. I'm glad to hear it. And

Bobbie's out with the Pavlov girl—and I'm glad of that, for once. But . . ."

"Oh," I said slowly, as if I was just beginning to see what he meant. "Look, Jim. Don't take this the wrong way, but where were you—"

"Quiet!" he said sharply. "I don't want to talk about it here."

"But, look," I said. "The time of death can't be fixed absolutely. So whether you—"

"I said I didn't want to talk about it here!" he snapped. "Can you meet me down in front of the courthouse in about fifteen minutes?"

"Why, sure," I said. "Even sooner. But—"

"Good! Do it, then."

He left. I went back out into the hall.

The nearest undertaking service was thirty miles away, so it would be some time before Luane's body could be removed. Sheriff Jameson agreed to stick around until the job was over; also to see that Ralph was taken care of comfortably for the night. He had one of his deputies put a couple of things of Ralph's into my car—things I was taking custody of temporarily—and then I left for town.

Jim Ashton was parked in front of the courthouse. He got out of his car as I drove up, started talking while I was still climbing out of mine.

"You asked me a question about fixing the time of death, Hank. Here's the answer. When a fatality is discovered as quickly as this one was, you can come damned close to fixing the time it occurred. Oh, you can't pin it down to a matter of minutes and seconds, but you can place it within a very narrow period. And, Hank, I can't account for my time during that period in this case!"

"But it was an accident," I said. "Anyway, you're not the only one who—"

"Who else is there? My son is in the clear. You and Lily are. Ralph is. There's that girl he's been chasing around with, of course, but if he's out of the picture she just about has to be, too. Anyway, she's in a lot better spot than I am.

And, damn her, it's her fault that I'm—but, let it go. The time of Luane's death can be placed within a certain period, and everyone but me can—"

"Just a minute." I put a hand on his arm. "Calm down, Jim. You were the one who examined Luane. What's to stop you from saying she died during a period that you can account for?"

He looked at me blankly. Jim's supposed to be a very intelligent man—and I'm sure he is—but he certainly couldn't keep up with me tonight. No one could have.

"Oh," he said, at last. "Why, yes, I guess I could, couldn't I?"

"Why not?" I winked and nudged him. "What's to stop you?"

A relieved smile spread over his face. Then he glanced over my shoulder, and the smile went away.

"There," he nodded grimly, and I turned around and looked. "That's what's to stop me!"

I'd expected Kossmeyer to be tipped off, and I knew he'd move fast as soon as he was. But I hadn't thought he would move this fast. And I hadn't planned on his doing what he had done—or, rather, what he was preparing to do.

His convertible was just about in the middle of the block, opposite us. Just passing under a streetlight. We could see him plain as day, and the man he had with him. The doctor who sometimes came here from out of town.

They passed on by, took the road that led toward the Devore place. Jim sighed and said, well, that was that, he guessed.

I told him I was sure everything would work out all right, but it didn't seem to help much. He drove away, still looking mighty sickish, and I took the stuff out of my car and carried it up to my office.

I was feeling a mite let-down myself. Kind of, you know, like someone had given me a little punch in the stomach. And it wasn't because I was worried about Jim. Jim hadn't killed Luane, I was positive of it. So unless he confessed—and I doubted if even Kossmeyer could break Jim Ashton down—he couldn't be convicted. He could be put to plenty of grief, of course; so much that he might just about as well be guilty as innocent. But—

Dammit, he almost deserved to be. If he hadn't been so careless or unlucky or dumb or something, I'd have had Kossmeyer against a stone wall. I could have put that little louse in his place, and made him like it.

I cussed, and took a kick at my wastebasket. I got busy on the telephone, trying to make the best of the situation. About thirty minutes passed. I'd just hung up after a call when the phone rang.

It was Jim. He had an alibi for the time of Luane's death, after all. Not only that, but the Lee girl also had one! They were each other's alibi!

I almost let out a war whoop when he told me the news. I think I would have if I hadn't glanced out the window and seen Kossmeyer coming up the walk.

I hung up the phone, thinking by God that this made everything perfect—hell, better than perfect!

I listened, grinning, as Kossmeyer came up the steps and down the hall. As he neared the door, I wiped off my grin and stood up.

I was very polite to him. Oh, extremely. I said it was a great honor to have such a distinguished visitor, and that I would feel privileged to assist him in any poor way that I could.

He looked a little startled, then embarrassed. Then, as he sat down across from me, he laughed sort of shyly. "I'm sorry," he said. "I just supposed that since we knew each other so well, and since it's pretty common practice to call in an outside doctor—"

"I'm delighted that you did," I said. "Nothing could have pleased me more. Now, as long as you're taking such an extraordinary interest in the case—"

"Extraordinary? It's extraordinary to be interested in the death of a client?"

"If you please," I said. "Perhaps if you will not interrupt we can conclude our business quickly. Now, I have here a canvas sack containing approximately fifty-seven thousand dollars. It belongs to Ralph Devore, and here is conclusive proof in the form of a ledger. I think you'll agree with me that—"

"Sure, I will," he nodded. "I'd sure as hell agree anyway that the guy could never be convicted. Luane couldn't have kept him from leaving her. He had no monetary motive for killing her. He was on the scene right about the time of her death, but— Yeah, counsellor? Go right ahead."

Go right ahead? Hell, there was hardly anything to go ahead with! I'd been all set to surprise him; I'd had it all planned. Just how he'd look and what he'd say, and what I'd say and—and everything. And then that damned stupid Jameson or one of his deputies had had to spoil it all.

"Well," I said, "as long as you've already been told . . ."

"Ought to have known without being told." He shook his head. "Ought to have been able to guess how things stood. On the other hand, who'd've ever thought that a guy like Devore would have that kind of dough? Or any considerable sum?"

"What's the difference?" I said. "It was his money. He certainly wouldn't have had to kill her to get his own money, would he?"

"You're quite right," he said gravely. "He would not have had to. I have no grounds for thinking that he did kill her— or, for that matter, that anyone did."

"You—" I paused. "You don't think that anyone did? You mean, you think it was an accident?"

"Well," he shrugged, "why not? There's that broken telephone line, of course, but you can't make anything out of that. Yeah, I'd be willing to let it go as an accident."

He looked at me, frowning a little. I looked down at my desk, feeling my face turn red, hardly knowing what to do or say next. He'd spoiled everything. Everything I'd planned to say, why—why, now I couldn't. All I could do was just sit there, like a bump on a log. Looking like a damned fool, and knowing that he thought I was one.

He cleared his throat. He murmured something about not

envying me my job, and a prosecutor's really having a hard row to hoe.

"Used to be on that side of the desk myself, y'know," he added. "Guess a lot of trial lawyers start off as prosecutors. Gives 'em all-around experience, and the longer they stick to it the better they get. You know what I always say, Mr. County Attorney? I say, you show me an experienced prosecutor, and I'll show you a topflight lawyer!"

I didn't say anything. I couldn't even make myself look up at him. He cleared his throat again.

"I'm afraid I've interrupted you so much that I've broken your chain of thought. Were you going to—uh— May I see that list?"

I shoved it toward him, the list of people who had a good reason for wanting Luane dead and who they had been with at the time of her death. He went down the double-column of names, murmuring aloud, kind of talking to himself but also speaking to me:

"Bobbie Ashton and Myra Pavlov . . . Lily and Henry C. Will— Oh, now, really. I hope you don't think that was necessary on my account . . . Doctor Ashton and Danny Lee. Hmm, hmm. Well, what the hell, though?"

He laid the list back on my desk. He murmured that I had certainly done a first-rate job of investigation; then, after a long awkward pause, he suddenly laughed.

My head came up. It was such a warm-sounding, friendly laugh that it was hard for me to keep from joining in.

"Y'know, Mr. County Attorney," he chuckled, "sometimes I feel like one of those characters in a Western movie. The guy that gets such an exaggerated reputation for toughness that he can't hardly tip his hat without someone thinking he's going for a gun. Sure, I try to take care of my clients, and maybe I'm overly conscientious about it. But I certainly don't go hunting for trouble. I don't like trouble, y'know? There's too damned much of it already without creating any."

He laughed again, giving me a sidewise glance, trying to draw me into his laughter. I looked back at him coldly—letting *him* squirm for a change, letting him feel as foolish as I had.

"Well—" He stood up awkwardly. "I guess—uh—I guess I'd better be going. See you around, huh? And my compliments on your thoroughness in handling this investigation."

He nodded, and started for the door. I let him get halfway there before I spoke.

"Just a moment, Mr. Kossmeyer . . ."

"Yeah?" He turned around.

"Come back here," I said. "I haven't told you you could leave yet."

"Wh-aat?" He laughed, kind of frowning. "What the hell is this?"

I stared at him silently. He came slowly back and again sat down across from me.

"You complimented me on my thoroughness," I said. "It suddenly occurred to me that I haven't been thorough enough. Where were you at the time of Luane Devore's death?"

"Where was—? Aw, now—"

"Luane said a great many ugly things about you. Whether they were true or not I don't know, but—"

"Then maybe we'd better stick to your question," he said quietly. "I was with my wife at the time."

"Oh? Your wife, eh?" I shook my head, kind of grinning down my nose. "Just your wife? You have no one else to support your story?"

"No one. There's only the one person. I'm in the same boat with those other people on your list—with you, for example."

"Well," I shrugged. "I suppose I'll have to accept that, then. I can't say that I'm completely satisfied, but—uh—"

His face had gone white. The pale had pushed up, spread over the summer's tan; and all his color seemed concentrated in his burning black eyes.

"Why ain't you satisfied?" he said. "What's there about me or my wife that makes our word less reliable than that of these other people?"

His voice was kind of a low, quivering purr. A kind of wound-up, coiled-tight undertone. He spoke again, repeating his question, and the quiver became stronger. The tenseness, the coiling seemed to extend to his body.

I began to get a little nervous, but I couldn't stop now. Not the way he was looking at me, the way he sounded: the way, in so many words, he was threatening me. If he'd just laughed again or even smiled a little; given me an opening to say, oh, hell, of course I was just joking . . .

"You've been kicking me in the teeth all evening," he said, "and I took it. But I ain't taking that last. When you tell me that my wife's word is no good—that she and I ain't as decent and upright as other people—then you throw the door wide open. You got a hell of a lot more tellin' to do then, buster, and by God you'd better not clown around when you do it. Because if you do—"

"Now, w-wait a minute," I said. "I—I—"

"What are you trying to cover up, Williams? Why did you go to such lengths to *prove* that this was an accident? You felt you had to, right? You had a guilty conscience, right? You knew—you sit there now, knowing that it was not an accident but murder. And knowing full well who the murderer is. That's right, isn't it, Williams? Answer me! You know who killed Luane Devore, and by God, I think I do, too! You've as good as admitted it. You've put the finger right on yourself! You've—"

"N-no! *NO!*" I said. "I w-was with my sister! I—"

"Suppose I told you I'd talked with your sister? Suppose I told you she's admitted that you weren't with her? Suppose I told you I've only been playing with you all evening—getting you out on a limb with this one-person alibi deal? Suppose . . ."

His voice had uncoiled; he had uncoiled. He was in front of me, leaning toward me, pounding on the desk. He was there, but he was also behind me, to the side of me, above me. He seemed to surround me like his voice, closing in, shutting out everything else. Chasing me further and further into a black, bewildering labyrinth where only he and the voice could follow. I couldn't think. I—I—

I thought, *Isn't it funny? How, when you feel so much one way, you act just the opposite?*

I thought, *She never said nothin'. Mama and Papa said I did real good . . . and she hated it. She hated me. All her life she's—*

"She did it!" It was me, screaming. "S-she said she was going to! S-she—she—she says I wasn't to home, why, she wasn't either! S-she—she—"

"Then she can't alibi for you, can she! You can't prove you were at home. And you weren't, were you, Williams? You were at the Devore house, weren't you, Williams? You were killing Luane, weren't you, Williams? Killing her and then faking—"

"*N-N-NO! NO!* Don't you s-see? I couldn't I—I couldn't hurt no one! H-honest, Mr. Kossmeyer! I—I ain't that way. I k-know it l-looks like—like—but that ain't me! I couldn't do it. I didn't, d-didn't, didn't, didn't . . ."

He was making little motions with his hands, motioning for me to stop. The whiteness was gone from his face, giving way to a deep flush. He looked ashamed and embarrassed, and kind of sick.

"I'm sorry," he said. "I didn't really think you killed Luane. I just got sore, and—"

"He didn't kill her," said a voice from the doorway. "I did."

XI

Myra Pavlov

PAPA JUST ABOUT scared me to death when he came home for lunch. He didn't act much different or say anything much more out of the way than he usually does—I guess he really didn't actually. But I kept feeling like he knew about Bobbie and me, and that that was why he was acting and talking the way he was. And finally I just got so nervous and scared that I jumped up from the table, and ran up to my room.

Afterwards, sitting up on the edge of my bed, I was scared even more. I thought, Oh, golly, now I *have* done it. Now, he *will* know there's something wrong, if he doesn't already. I shivered and shook. I began to get sick to my stomach; kind of a morning sickness like I've had a lot lately. But I didn't dare go to the bathroom. He might hear me, and come upstairs. He might start asking Mama questions, and that would be just as bad, because she's even scareder of him than I am.

It's funny how we feel about him; I mean, the way we're always so scared of him. Because there's actually no real reason to be. He's never hit Mama or me. He's never threatened us or cussed us out. He's never done anything of the things that mean men are supposed to do to their families, and yet we've always been scared of him. Almost as far back as I can remember, anyway.

Well, after a moment or so, Mama left the table too, and came upstairs, stopped in the doorway of my room. I held my hand over my mouth and pointed. She pointed to my shoes. I slipped them off, and followed her down the hall to the bathroom. And, golly, was it a relief to get in there.

I used the sink to vomit in, and Mama kept running the water to cover up the noise. It was sure a relief.

We went back to my room, she in her shoes and me in my stocking feet. We sat down on my bed, and she put her arms around me and held me. She was kind of stiff and awkward about it, since we've never done much kissing and hugging or anything like that in our family. But it was nice, just the same.

It wasn't much later, but it seemed like hours before Papa left. Mama's arms slid away from me and we both heaved a big sigh. And then we laughed, kind of weakly, because it was sort of funny, you know.

"How are you feeling, girl?" Mama said. "Girl" is about as close as she ever comes to calling me a pet name. I said I was feeling pretty good now.

"Stand up and let me take a look at you," Mama said.

I stood up. I pulled my dress up above my waist, and Mama looked at me. Then, she motioned for me to sit down again.

"It doesn't show none at all," she said. "You couldn't tell there's a thing wrong by looking at you. Of course, it wouldn't need to show if he's—he's—"

"Do you think he has, Mama?" I started to tremble a little. "Y-you don't think he has heard anything, do you, Mama?"

"Well, sure, now," Mama said quickly. "Of course he hasn't. I reckon he'd sure let us know if he had."

"But—but what makes him act so funny then?"

"Mean, you mean," Mama said. "When did he ever act any other way?"

She sat, turning her hands in her lap, looking down at the big blue veins in the rough red flesh. Her legs were bare, and they were red and rough, too; bruised-looking where the varicose veins were broken. She was just kind of a mass of redness and roughness, from her face to her feet. And all at once I began to cry.

"There, there, girl," she said, giving me an awkward pat. "Want me to get you something to eat?"

"N-no." I shook my head.

She said I'd better eat; I'd hardly touched my lunch. She said she could bake me up something real quick—some puff bread or something else real tasty.

"Oh, Mama." I wiped my eyes, suddenly smiling a little. "That's all you ever think of! I'll bet if a person had a broken leg you'd try to feed them!"

"Well . . ." She smiled, kind of embarrassed. "I guess I would probably, at that."

"Well," I said. "I guess I could probably eat a couple of those fresh crullers you made this morning. Maybe a couple of cups of good strong coffee, too. All at once, I'm actually really pretty hungry, Mama."

"You know, I kind of am myself, girl," Mama said. "You just stay here and rest, and I'll bring us up a bite."

She brought up some coffee and a half-dozen crullers, and a couple of big thick potroast sandwiches. We were both pretty full when we finished—at least, I couldn't have eaten anything more. And I felt kind of peaceful, dull peaceful, you know, like you do when you're full.

A fly buzzed against the screen. A nice little breeze drifted through the window, bringing the smell of alfalfa blossoms. I guess nothing smells quite as good as alfalfa, unless it's fresh-baked bread. I wondered why Mama wasn't baking today, because she almost always puts dough to set on Sunday night, and bakes bread on Monday.

"Guess I just didn't have the will for it," she said, when I asked her about it. "You bake all day in this weather, and it takes the house a week to cool off."

"It wouldn't if you cooked with gas," I said. "You ought to make him put in gas, Mama!"

Mama made a sort of sour-funny face. She asked me if I'd ever known of anyone to make Papa do anything. "Anyway," she added, slowly. "I don't think he's burning coal any more just to bother the neighbors."

I said that, well, I thought so. I *knew* so. "Why did you ever marry him anyway, Mama? You must have known what he was like. There certainly must have been some signs of it."

"Well . . ." She brushed a wisp of hair back from her forehead. "I told you the why of it about a hundred times already, girl. He was older than me, so he got out of the orphanage first. And then he started dropping back to visit, after he was making money, so . . ."

"But you just didn't marry him to get away from the place?" I said. "That wasn't the only reason, was it?"

"No, of course not," Mama said.

"He was different then, Mama? You were in love with him?"

She looked down in her lap again, twisting her hands. Words like "love" always embarrass Mama, and her face was a little flushed.

"It wasn't the only reason I married him," she said. "Just to get away from the orphanage. But maybe . . . I kind of think maybe he thought it was. We shouldn't talk about him like we do, girl. Shouldn't even think things like we do. He's pretty sensitive, you know, quick to catch on to what someone else is thinkin', and—"

"Well, it's his own fault," I said. "What else can he expect, anyway?"

Mama shook her head. She didn't say anything.

"Mama," I said. "What did you mean a minute ago when you said Papa probably couldn't have the house piped for gas, even if he wanted to? You didn't mean he didn't have the money, did you?"

"No, of course, not. I didn't mean anything—just thinking nonsense and I said it out loud," Mama said quickly.

"Don't you ever breathe a word around about your Papa not having money, girl."

I said I wouldn't. In the first place it would be silly and a lie; and then it would make Papa awfully mad. "He's got all kinds of money," I said, "and, Mama, I just g-got to—"

I started crying again. Right out of a clear blue sky without any warning.

"I can't stand it any longer!" I said. "I'm getting so scared, and—could you get some money from him, Mama? Make him give you enough for me and Bobbie to—"

I didn't finish the question. It was too foolish. I wouldn't even have started to ask it if I hadn't been half-scared to death.

"I don't know why he has to be so hateful!" I said. "If he wants to—to— Why doesn't he do something to that dirty old Luane Devore? She's the one that's causing all the trouble!"

"There, there, girl," Mama mumbled. "No use in getting yourself—"

"Well, why doesn't he?" I said. "Why doesn't he do something to her?"

"He wouldn't see no call to," Mama said. "As long as it was the truth, why, Papa wouldn't . . ."

She frowned, her voice trailing off into silence. I spoke to her a couple times, saying that it wasn't fair and that I just couldn't go on any longer. But she didn't say anything back to me.

Finally, when I was about ready to yell, I was getting so nervous, she sighed and shook her head.

"I . . . I guess not, girl. I thought I had a notion about some place I might get some money for you, but I guess I can't."

"But maybe I could!" I said. "Bobbie and me! Who—"

"You keep out of it," Mama said sharply. "You couldn't get it, even if it could be got. I thought for a moment I might get, part of it anyway, because I'm your Papa's wife. But—"

"But I could try!" I said. "Please, Mama! Just tell me who it is, and—"

"I told you you couldn't get it," Mama said, "and trying wouldn't get you anything but trouble. This party would tell Papa about it, and you know what would happen then."

"Well..." I hesitated. "I guess you're probably right, Mama. If you couldn't get it, why, I don't see how I could. Is it an old debt someone owes Papa?"

Mama said it was kind of a debt. It was and it wasn't. And there was no way that the party could be forced to pay it.

"For one thing," she added, "the party's got no money to pay with that I know of. Papa thinks different—I kind of got the notion he does from some things he's let slip—but you know him. Someone says something is white, why, he'll say it's black, just to be contrary."

"I just can't imagine," I said. "I just can't see Papa letting someone get away without paying him what they owe."

"I told you," Mama said. "They—this party don't really owe it. I mean, they do and they ought to pay, but—"

"Tell me who it is, Mama," I said. "Please, *please,* Mama. I—I've got to do something. I c-can't be any worse off than I am now. If you won't see the party, do anything to help me, at least—"

"I can't, girl." Mama bit her lip. "You know I would if—"

"Can't what?" I said. "You can't help me, or you can't let me help myself?"

"I—I just..." She pushed herself to her feet, started loading dishes back onto the tray. "I'll tell you how you can help yourself," she said, looking hurt and sullen. "You can just stay away from that Bobbie Ashton until he's ready to marry you."

I started crying again, burying my face in my hands. I said, what good would that do, for heaven's sake. Bobbie might get mad or interested in someone else. Anyway, even if I did stop seeing him, it wouldn't change anything when Papa found out about us.

"You k-know I'm right, Mama," I sobbed. "H-he'd still —he'll kill us, Mama! H-he's going to kill me, and—and I've got no one to turn to. You won't h-help me, a-and you

w-won't let me do anything. All you can do is just fuss
around and mumble, a-and ask m-me if I want something to
eat, a-and—"

The dishes rattled on the tray. One of the cups toppled
over into its saucer. Then, I heard her turn and shuffle toward the door.

"All right, girl," she said, dully. "I'll do it tonight."

"M-Mama—" I took my hands away from my face. "You
know I didn't mean what I said, Mama."

"It's all right," Mama said. "You didn't say anything that
wasn't true."

"But I didn't—you'll do what, Mama?"

"I'll see that party tonight. It won't do no good, I'm pretty
sure, but I'll do it."

She went on out of the room, and down the stairs. I sat
forward on the bed, studying myself in the dresser mirror. I
certainly looked a fright. My eyes were all red and my face
blotched, and my nose swollen up like a sweet potato. I
hadn't put up my hair last night either. And now, what with
the heat and my nervous sweating, it was as limp and drab-
looking as a dishrag.

I went to the bathroom, soaked my face in cold water and
dabbed it with astringent. Then, I took a nice long lukewarm
bath, putting up my hair as I sat in the tub.

I tried to tell myself that I hadn't said anything out of the
way to Mama, that she'd certainly never done much of anything else for me, and that it was no more than right that she
should do this. I told myself that—those things—and I
guess there was a lot of truth to it. But still I began to feel
awful bad—awful ashamed of myself. She'd always done as
much for me as she could, I guessed. It wasn't her fault that
Papa had just about taken everything out of her that she had
to do with.

There was last spring, for example, when I graduated
from high school; she'd gone way out on a limb to help me
then. To try to help me, I should say. I'd told her that she
simply couldn't let Papa come to the graduation exercises.
I'd simply *die* if he did, I told her, because none of the other

kids had any use for me now, and if he came it would be ten times worse.

"You know how it'll be, Mama," I said, kind of crying and storming. "He won't be dressed right, and he'll go around snorting and sneering and being sarcastic to the other parents, and—and just acting as awful as he knows how! I just won't go if he goes, Mama! I'd be so embarrassed I'd sink right through the floor!"

Well, Mama mumbled and massaged her hands together and looked bewildered. She said it really wasn't right for me to feel that way about Papa; and maybe she could drop him a few hints so that he'd look nice and behave himself.

"I don't hardly know what else I can do," she said. "He means to go, and I don't see how—"

"I told you how, Mama!" I said. "You can pretend like you're sick, and you don't want to be left alone. You can do it just as well as not, and you know it!"

Mama mumbled and massaged her hands some more. She said she guessed she could do what I was asking, but she'd sure hate to. "He'd be awfully disappointed, girl. He'd try to cover it up, but he would be."

"I just bet he would!" I said. "Naturally, he'd be disappointed missing a chance to make me feel nervous and cheap. I just can't stand it if he goes, Mama!"

"But it means so much to him, girl," Mama said. "You see, he hardly had any education himself, not even as much as I did. Now, to have his own daughter graduating from high school, why—"

"Oh, pooh!" I said. "I won't go if he goes, Mama! I'll run away from home! I'll—I'll k-kill myself! I'll . . ."

I really ranted and raved on. I'd been feeling awfully upset and nervous anyway, because I'd just started going with Bobbie Ashton at the time, and he wasn't nice to me like he is now, and—but never mind that. That was a long time ago, and I don't like to think it ever even happened. Anyway, to get back to the subject, I kept insisting that Papa just couldn't go to the graduation exercises. I ranted and raved and cried until finally Mama gave in.

She agreed to play sick, and keep Papa at home.

She was upstairs in bed that evening when he came in. I was out in the kitchen, getting dinner ready. I heard him come through the living room and dining room. I could feel those eyes of his boring into the back of my neck as he stood in the kitchen doorway. He didn't say anything. Just stood there staring at me. I dropped a spoon to the floor, I was so nervous and scared, and when I picked it up I had to turn away from the stove. Facing him.

I really didn't recognize him for a second, actually. I really didn't. He'd changed clothes down at the pavilion, and the way he was dressed now, well, I just didn't think he *could* be. I'd never seen him look like this before . . . and I never did again.

He was wearing a brand new blue suit, a real stylish one. He had on a new hat, too—a gray Homburg—and new black dress shoes—the first he'd ever worn, I guess—and a new white shirt, and a tie that matched his suit. He looked so smart and kind of distinguished that I actually didn't know him for a second. I was so surprised that I almost forgot to be scared.

"W-why—why, Papa," I stammered. "Why—where—"

He grinned, looking embarrassed. "Stopped by a rummage sale," he said gruffly. "Picked this up while I was there, too."

He pushed a little package at me. I fumbled it open, and there was a velvet box inside. And inside the box was a wristwatch. A platinum wristwatch with diamonds in it.

I stared at it; I told him thank you, I guess. But if I'd had the nerve I'd've told him something else. I might have even thrown the watch at him.

You see, I'd been hinting for a watch for months—hinting as much as a person dares to with Papa. And all he'd ever do was just laugh or grunt and laugh at me. He'd say things like, well, what the hell do you want a watch for? Or, what you need is a good alarm clock. Or, them damned wristwatches ain't nothing but junk.

That's the way he talked, acted, and all the time he was planning to buy me a watch.

All the time he was planning on buying these new clothes, dressing himself up so people would hardly know him.

"Here's something else," he said, tossing a glassine-topped box on the table. A box with an orchid in it. "Stole it out at the graveyard."

I said thank you again—I guess. I was so mixed up, mad and not mad—kind of ashamed—and nervous and scared, that I don't know what I said. Or whether I actually said anything, really.

"Where's your mother?" he said. "Didn't throw herself out with the trash, did she?"

"S-she's upstairs," I said. "She-she's l-lying—"

"Lyin' about what?" He laughed; broke off suddenly. "What's the matter? Spit it out! She ain't sick, is she?"

I nodded, said, yes, that she was sick. I'd been working myself up to saying it all day, and now it just popped out before I could stop it.

Anyway, what else could I have said? Mama wouldn't know that I didn't want her to play sick now—that I'd just as soon she didn't. If I tried to change our story, it might get her into trouble with Papa. Get us both in trouble.

Well, naturally I looked awfully pale and dragged-out. And, of course, he thought I looked that way on account of Mama. He cursed, turned a little pale himself.

"What's the matter with her?" he said. "When'd she take sick? Why didn't you call me? What'd the Doc say about her?"

"N-nothing," I stammered. "I—I d-don't think she's very sick, Papa."

"Think?" he said. "You mean you ain't called the doctor? Your mother's sick in bed, and— For God's sake!"

He ran to the hall telephone, and called Doctor Ashton. Told him to get over to the house as fast as he could. Then he started upstairs, hurrying but kind of dragging his feet, too.

The doctor arrived. Papa came back downstairs, and out

into the kitchen where I was. He paced back and forth, nervously, cursing and grumbling and asking questions.

"Goddammit," he said, "you ought to have called me. You ought to've called the doctor right away. I don't know why the hell you—"

"P-Papa," I said. "I d-don't think— I mean, I'm sure she's not very sick."

"How the hell would you know?" He cursed again. Then he said, "What the hell does she have to go and get sick for? She ain't had a sick day in twenty years, so why does she got to do it now?"

"Papa . . ."

"She better cut it out, by God," he said. "She gets sick on me, I'll put her in a hospital. Make her stay there until I say she can leave. Get some real doctors to look after her, and— Yeah? Dammit, if you got something to say, say it!"

I tried to say it, to tell him the truth. But I didn't get very far. He broke in, cursing, when I said Mama wasn't really sick; then he stopped scolding and cursing and said, well, maybe I was right: sure, she wasn't really sick.

"Probably just over-et," he said. "Probably just been workin' too hard . . . That's about the size of it, don't you think so, Myra? Couldn't be nothin' serious, could it?"

"No, Papa," I said. "P-Papa, I keep trying to tell you—"

"Why, sure, sure," he said. "We're—you're getting all upset over nothing. You just calm down now, and everything will be fine. There's not a thing in the world to worry about. Doc will get Mama up on her feet, and we'll all go to the graduation together, and— Now cut out that goddamn bawling, will you? You sound like a calf in a hailstorm."

"P-Papa," I sobbed. "Oh, Papa, I j-just feel so bad that—"

"Well, you just cut it out," he said, "because there ain't a damned lick of sense to it. Mama's going to be just dandy, and—an'—"

Doctor Ashton was coming down the stairs. Papa kind of swallowed, and then went out to the foot of the staircase to meet him.

"How—how is she, Doc?" I heard him say. "Is she—?"

"Your wife," Doctor Ashton said, "is in excellent physical condition for a woman her age. She is as healthy as the proverbial horse."

Papa let out a grunt. I could almost see his eyes clouding over like they do when he's angry. "What the hell you talkin' about, anyway? What kind of a doctor are you? My wife's—"

"Your wife is not sick. She has not been sick," said Doctor Ashton, and, ooh, did he sound mean! He had everything pretty well figured out, I guess, and the way he dislikes Papa it tickled him to death. "That's a very handsome outfit you're wearing, Pavlov. I take it that you planned on attending the graduation exercises tonight."

"Well, sure. Naturally," Papa said. "Now, what do you mean—"

"It must have come as quite a surprise to your family." The screen door opened, and Doctor Ashton stepped out on the porch. "Yes, quite a surprise. The apparel, that is, not your plans for attending the exercises."

Papa said, "Now, listen, goddammit. What—" Then he said, "Oh." Just the one word, slowly, dully.

"Yes," the doctor said. "Well, there's no reason at all why you can't attend, Pavlov. None at all. That is, of course, if you still want to."

He laughed softly. He went on out to his car, and drove away. And minutes later, it seemed like I could still hear that laugh of his.

I waited in the kitchen, stood right where I had been standing. Not moving, except for the trembling. Hardly even breathing.

And Papa stayed out in the hallway. Not moving either, it seemed. Just standing and waiting, like I was standing and waiting.

I was sure he was just working up to an explosion. Putting all the mean ugly things together in his mind, so he could cloud up and rain all over me and Mama. That was what he was going to do, I was sure, because he'd done the same thing before. Made us wait, you know. Wait and wait, knowing that he was going to do something and getting so jumpy we were about to fall apart. And then suddenly cutting loose on us.

I wished that he'd cut loose now, and get it over with. I wished he'd just do it, you know; not because it was so hard to go on waiting, but because it would kind of even things up. And maybe he'd stop feeling the way he must be feeling now.

It sounds funny—or, no, I guess it doesn't—but I'd never really cared about how he felt before. I mean, I'd never actually thought about his having any feelings—about being able to hurt his feelings. Because you'd never have thought it from the way he'd always acted. He'd always gone out of his way to show that he didn't care how anyone felt about him or acted toward him, so . . .

Maybe Mama is right. She was an awfully pretty girl back when she married Papa, and Papa was kind of short and stocky like he is now, and about as homely as a mud fence. So, since she never could express herself very well and she's always been so kind of frozen-faced and shy—just embarrassed all to pieces just by the mention of love or anything like that—why, maybe Papa did think she married him just to get away from the orphanage. And maybe that's the reason, partly the reason, anyway—

Oh, I don't know. And the way things are now, I couldn't care less. Because he certainly doesn't care anything about me, even if he might have at one time.

How could he—a father that would actually kill his own daughter if he found out a certain thing about her?

Bobbie says I have things all wrong; Papa would do it because he cares so much. But that just doesn't make any sense, does it, and as sweet and smart as Bobbie is, he can say some awfully foolish things.

Well, anyway, getting back to that night:

Papa didn't do what I expected him to. He started for the kitchen once, but he stopped after a step or two. Then he took a couple of steps toward the stairs, and stopped again.

Finally, he went to the screen door and pushed it open, paused with one foot inside the house and the other on the porch.

"Got to go back to the office," he called. "Won't want any supper. Won't be able to go to the graduation. You and Mama have a good—you two watch out for the squirrels."

I called, "P-Papa—wait!" But the screen door slammed, drowning out the words.

By the time I got to the door, he was a block up the street.

He never wore those clothes again. I saw Goofy Gannder in the Homburg one day, so I guess Papa probably gave him the whole outfit, and Goofy traded the other things for booze.

Well, as I was saying, Mama really had tried to help me that one time, at least, and it wasn't fair to say that she hadn't. Also, as I was about to say, it wasn't very nice of me to get her to try anything again. She'd have to face Papa afterwards. He'd take out on her what he couldn't take out on me, and an old woman like that—she was forty-six her last birthday—she just wouldn't be able to take it.

Aside from that, it probably wouldn't do any good; I mean, she probably wouldn't get away with whatever she was thinking about doing. She'd be so scared and unsure of herself that she'd make a botch of it, get herself into a lot of trouble without making me any better off than I was now.

So . . . so I finished putting up my hair, and went back to my bedroom. I put on a robe, went downstairs and told Mama I was sorry about the way I talked to her.

She didn't answer me; just turned away looking hurt, sullen-hurt. I put my arms around her and kissed her, and tried to pet her a little. That got her all red-faced and embarrassed, and kind of broke the ice.

"It's all right, girl," she said. "I don't blame you for being upset, and I'll do what I said I would."

"No, Mama," I said. "I don't want you to. Honestly, I don't. After all, you said you were sure it wouldn't do any good, so why take chances for nothing?"

"Well, I'm pretty sure that it wouldn't—that I couldn't get any money from this party. But . . ." She paused, relieved that I was letting her off, but a little suspicious along with it. "Look, girl. You're not planning on—on—"

"On what?" I laughed. "Now, what in the world could I do, Mama? Hold up a bank?"

Actually, I wasn't planning on doing anything. The idea didn't come to me until later, when I went back upstairs. It seems kind of funny that I hadn't thought of it before— under the circumstances, I mean—but I guess it actually really wasn't so strange. I just hadn't been desperate enough until now.

"So you just forget all about it, Mama," I said. "Don't do anything tonight, anyway. If something else doesn't turn up in a few days, why—"

"But I'll have to do it tonight, girl! Have to if I'm goin' to at all."

"Why do you?" I said. "If it's waited all these years, why can't it wait a little longer?"

"Because it can't! This party's telephone will—will—"

She broke off abruptly, turning to stir something on the stove. "My heavens, girl! I get to jabbering with you, and I'll burn up everything in the house."

"What about the telephone, Mama?" I said. "What were you going to say?"

"Nothing. How do I know, anyway?" Mama said. "Lord, what a day! I'm getting so rattled I don't know what I'm saying."

I laughed, and said I wouldn't worry again. I told her I really didn't want her to see the party she'd mentioned— that I'd really be very angry if she did. And she nodded and mumbled, so that took care of that.

I went back up to my room. I took off my robe, put on some fresh underthings and stretched out on the bed. It was nice and cool. I'd left the bedroom door open, and the draft sucked the alfalfa-smelling breeze through the window.

I closed my eyes, really relaxing for about the first time all day. My mind seemed to go completely empty for a moment—just cleared out of everything. And then all sorts of things, images, began to drift through it:

Mama ... Papa ... Bobbie ... the pavilion ... Me ... Me going into the pavilion. Unlocking the ticket booth. Going into Daddy's office, and opening the safe. Taking out the change box, and—

My eyes popped open, and I sat up suddenly. Then, I remembered that this was Monday, that there wouldn't be any dance tonight so I wouldn't have to work.

I sighed, and started to lay back down again.

I sat back up, slowly, feeling my eyes get wider and wider. Feeling my stomach sort of squeeze together inside, then gradually unsqueeze.

I got my purse off the dresser. I took out my key ring, stared at it for a moment and dropped it back in the purse.

It was almost four o'clock. I undid my hair, even though it had only been up a little while, and then I began to dress.

Mama came upstairs while I was putting my face on. She started to go on by to her own room, but she saw me dressed and fixing my face, so she turned back and came in. She asked me where in the world I thought I was going at this time of day.

"Oh, I thought I'd meet Bobbie in town tonight," I said. "I think it might be better than having him come here to the house, if people are doing any talking."

"But it ain't tonight yet," Mama said. "You haven't even had your supper yet. What—"

"I don't want any supper, Mama," I said. "Heavens, I just go through stuffing myself just a little while ago, didn't I? Anyway, the real reason I want to leave early is so I won't have to see Papa. I just can't face him again so soon, after the way he acted at lunch."

Mama started getting nervous. She said Papa would be sure to wonder about my being away at supper time, and what was she going to tell him?

I turned around from the mirror, looking pretty exasperated, I guess, because I certainly felt that way.

"Why, for heavens sake, just tell him the truth, Mama," I

said. "I mean, tell him I ate late and I didn't want any supper—dinner—so I just went on into town. I'll just walk around or drink a malted or something until it's time to meet Bobbie. Good grief, there's nothing wrong with that, is there? Can't I even go downtown without explaining and arguing and arguing and explaining until—"

"What you getting so excited about, girl?" Mama looked at me suspiciously. "You up to something?"

I drew in my breath real deep, giving her a good hard stare. And then I turned back to the mirror again.

"Look, girl," Mama mumbled, apologetically. "I'm just worried about you. If you've got some notion of—well, I don't know what you might be thinking about doing. But—"

"Mama," I said. "I'm going to get awfully mad in a minute."

"But, girl. You just can't—"

"All right, Mama," I said. "All right! I've argued and explained just as much as I'm going to, and now I'm not going to say another word. Not another word, Mama! I told you why I was leaving early. I told you I couldn't bear to face Papa tonight, and I can't. I simply *can't,* Mama, and there's no reason why I should, and I haven't the slightest intention of making the slightest effort to do so, and—and I'm not going to say another word about it, and I don't want to hear another word about it!"

She twitched, and rubbed her hands together. I'll bet they wouldn't be so red and big-veined if she wasn't always rubbing them together. She started to argue again, but I told her I'd cry if she did. So that stopped her right at the start.

"Well," she mumbled, "you're going to drink a cup of coffee first, anyway. I'm not going to let you leave this house without at least something hot on your stomach."

"Oh, Mama," I sighed. "Well, hurry up and get it, if you're going to! I can't drink it after I put my lipstick on."

She hurried downstairs, and brought me up some coffee. I drank it, and started fixing my mouth.

She watched me, twitching and massaging her hands. I caught her eye in the mirror, gave her a good hard look, believe me, and she shifted her eyes quickly. She didn't look at me again until I was all through.

"Well," I said, "I guess I'd better run along, now, if I want to miss Papa."

"All right, girl." She got up from the bed where she'd been sitting. "Take care of yourself, now, and don't stay out too late."

She started to kiss me good-bye; and that was kind of funny, you know, because she doesn't go in much for kissing. I pretended I didn't know what she meant to do, turning my head so as not to get my face smeared.

After all, I didn't have time to fix it again, did I? And if she wanted to kiss someone, why did she have to wait until they were in a hurry and all ready to go somewhere?

"Girl," she said, nervously. "I don't want you getting upset again, but—promise me, girl! Promise you won't—"

"Now, Mama, I *have* promised," I said. "I've told you and told you, and I'm not going to tell you again. Now, will you please stop harping on the subject?"

"You don't have to do anything, girl! I'll go—I'll think of something. Something's bound to turn up."

"Well, *all right!*" I said. "All right, for heaven's sake!"

And I snatched up my purse, and left.

She called after me, but I kept right on going, down the stairs and out the door. Then, as I was going out the gate, she called to me again—waved to me from the bedroom window. So, well, I gave her a smile and waved back.

I honestly wasn't mad, you know, and naturally I didn't mean to do anything that would make her feel bad. It was just that I had so much on my mind, that I simply couldn't stand any more.

It was a little after five when I got downtown, about five-fifteen. I wanted Papa to get clear home before I went to his office, so that meant I had almost forty-five minutes to kill. Well, thirty-five minutes, anyway, figuring that it would take ten minutes to walk down to the pavilion.

I sauntered around the courthouse square a couple of times, looking in the store windows. I stopped in front of the jewelry store, pretending like I was interested in the jewelry display, but actually looking at myself in the big panel-mirrors behind it.

I thought I looked pretty good tonight, considering all I'd been through. I honestly looked especially good in spite of everything.

I had on a white cashmere sweater I'd bought two weeks before—I guessed it wasn't rushing the season too much to wear it. I had on a new blue flannel skirt, and extra-sheer stockings and my practically new handmade suede shoes.

I studied myself in the mirror, thinking that whatever else you could say about him, you certainly couldn't say he was stingy. Mama and I could buy just about anything we wanted to, and he'd never say a word. All he ever insisted on was that we pay cash.

Mama always kept a hundred dollars cash on hand. As far back as I could remember, she did. Whenever she or I bought anything, why, she'd tell him, and he'd give her enough to bring her back up to a hundred dollars.

Actually, she—or I should say, I—hadn't spent much until this summer. I was actually scared to death of going in a store; afraid, you know, that the clerks might be laughing at me or talking about me behind my back. And Mama was even worse than I was. We never bought anything until we just had to. When we couldn't put it off any longer, we'd just take the first thing that was showed to us and practically run out of the place.

Papa just talked awful about us. I never will forget some of the mean things he said. He said he'd rent Mama out as a scarecrow, if it wouldn't've been so hard on the crows. And he said I looked like a leaky sack of bran that was about to fall over.

Well, he certainly hasn't had any cause to talk that way since I started going with Bobbie. Not about me, anyhow. I simply couldn't look dowdy around Bobbie, so I just *made* myself shop like a person should. And after I'd done it a few times, I didn't mind it at all. I mean, I actually really liked it, and I really *did* do some shopping from then on.

Nowadays, I hardly ever go into town without buying something.

Why not, anyway? Papa has plenty of money. If he can't treat me decent, why, at least he can let me *look* decent.

I glanced at my wristwatch, saw that it was getting close to six. I started for the pavilion, walking fast. Wondering how much money there'd be in his strongbox.

I never touched the strongbox ordinarily. I had no reason to, in my ticket-selling job, so I didn't know how much was in it. But I knew there'd be a lot. Papa didn't do any business with the banks that he didn't absolutely have to. He'd always paid "cash on the barrelhead," as he says, for practically everything. And when you have as many interests as Papa, that takes a lot of cash.

Of course, the dance business had fallen off quite a bit, and some of his other things weren't doing so well. But, goodness, what of it? Look at all the property he owned! Look at all the money he'd made when business was good! Papa could lose money for years, and he'd still be rich. Everyone in town said so. Maybe there wouldn't be as much in the strongbox as there used to be, but there'd still be plenty. Two or three thousand dollars, at least.

I was about a half block from the pavilion when I saw Ralph Devore come out of the rear exit, and climb up into the air-conditioner shed.

I stopped dead in my tracks. I thought, Oh, golly, how *could* I have forgot about him? Why does he had to be working all the time? I was actually sick for a moment, I was so disappointed. Then, I just tossed my head and kept right on going. Because it suddenly dawned on me that it didn't make a bit of difference whether Ralph was there or not. Even if he saw me, which wasn't likely, it wouldn't matter.

Ralph wouldn't think anything of my going into Papa's office. After all, I was the owner's daughter, and it just wouldn't occur to him to try to stop me or ask me what I was doing. Of course, he'd talk later when Papa missed the money, but I didn't care about that. Bobbie and I would be gone by that time, and we'd never come back.

I went through the door of the pavilion. I started across the floor, my knees just a little shaky. Ralph was pounding on something back in the air-conditioner shed—hammering on something. The noise came out through the ballroom air-vents, *thud-bang*, *thud-bang*, and I kind of walked—marched—in time to it.

My feet began to drag. That crazy pounding, it was just awful; it made me feel like I was in a funeral procession or something. And it kept right on going on, after it *wasn't* going on. I mean, I realized suddenly that Ralph wasn't pounding any more, and all that noise was coming from my heart.

I took a deep breath. I told myself to stop acting so silly, because there just wasn't any sense to it.

Bobbie and I would be a long way from here in another hour. Papa would know I'd taken his money—I wanted him to know it! But he wouldn't be able to catch up with us himself, and he'd never call on the police. He'd have too much pride to let anyone know that his own daughter had stolen from him.

I was at the door of his office. I opened my purse and took out my keys, fumbled through them until I found the right one.

I unlocked the door. I stepped inside, closed it behind me, and flicked on the light. And screamed.

Because Papa was there.

He was sitting at his desk, his face buried in his arms. There was a half-full bottle of whiskey in front of him.

He sat up with a start when I screamed. He jumped up, cursing, asking me what the hell was the idea, and so on. And then when I just stood staring at him, my mouth hanging open, he slowly sat down again. And stared at me.

Ralph came running across the ballroom floor. He stopped in the doorway of the office, and asked if something was wrong. Papa didn't say anything, even look at him. Ralph said, "Oh, uh, excuse me," and went away again.

Papa and I went on staring at each other.

He didn't need to ask why I was here. He knew. I'd've bet

a million dollars that he did. He'd been scheming and planning all along, figuring out ways to get me so scared and desperate that I'd finally try this. And then, when I did try, when he'd let me get my hopes all up, thinking that I'd found a way out...

Oh, he knew all right! He'd planned it this way. What else would he be doing there if he hadn't? Why hadn't he gone on home to supper like he always did?

I backed toward the door. I thought, *Oh, how I hate you! HOW I HATE YOU! I hate you so much that—that—! I hate you, hate you, hate you!*

Papa nodded. "Figured you probably did," he said. "Well, you got a lot of company."

I turned and ran.

It didn't occur to me until later that I must have said what I was thinking. That I'd actually yelled it at him.

XII

Pete Pavlov

I'D GOTTEN THE letter from Doc Ashton the week before. I didn't answer it, so that Monday he phoned me. I told him to go to hell and hung up.

Only thing to do, as I saw it. And wrong or right, a man's got to go by what he sees. He's got a chance that way. It's a lot handier for him. Any time a butt needs kicking, he knows whose it is.

I punched out a few letters on my old three-row typewriter. I carried them down to the post-office, thinking that they didn't make typewriters like they used to. Thinking that they didn't make nothing like they used to, from bread to chewing tobacco. Then, kind of snorting to myself and thinking, Well, by God, look who's talking! Maybe they don't make nothing like they used to because there's no one to do the making. Nothing but a lot of whining old guys with weep-bags in place of guts.

I guessed I must be slipping. If I'd been like this back at the time I built the post-office building... *Well, maybe it would've been a hell of a lot better, I thought. I wouldn't be in the spot I'm in now, and there'd be quite a few less bastards around town to give me trouble.*

Yeah, the post-office job was mine. Built it under contract for old Commodore Stuyvesant, Luane Devore's father. It's still the biggest building in town—four stories—and it was a pretty fancy one for those days. The upper three floors were offices, each with its own toilet and lavatory. All the plumbing, the water and drain pipes, was concealed.

Well, we were about through with the job, except for the interior decorating, when I discovered a hell of a thing. I'll never forget the day that it happened. I was up on the fourth floor at the time. I'd taken the chaw out of my mouth and tossed it in the toilet. Then I'd flushed it down and drawn myself a drink from the lavatory. And I was just about to toss it down when I noticed something in the water. A few little brown specks, so tiny you could hardly see them.

I cussed, and dumped out the water. I got myself a can of stain, and went through the building from top to bottom, flushing toilets and turning on faucets. They all turned out the same as the first. They were all cross-connected, to use the plumbing term. You had to be looking for the stain in the water, and looking damned hard, but it was there. Some of the waste water was coming out through the lavatory taps.

You see . . . Well, you know what the inside of a toilet bowl looks like. It has a water inlet built into it; it has to have a flush; and it also has a sewage outlet. It has the two right together, flowing together. If the plumbing ain't exactly right, some of the sewage can get into the water inlet. Into the water you drink and wash with.

Well, the first thing I did was to cut off the water at the main. Shut off every drop in the building. I told the workmen they'd been screwing around too much on the job, that they could do their washing and drinking on their own time from now on. And they didn't exactly love me for that, naturally. But it was the way it had to be. I couldn't tell them the truth. If I had, it would have got all over town. People would always have been leery of the building. You could fix the trouble, and take an oath on it, but they'd never really believe that you had.

I spent the rest of the day checking the blueprints on the job, tracing out the miles of piping foot by foot. Finally, I spotted what was wrong. It was in the blueprints, the drawings, themselves. Not something that was my fault.

I took the drawings, and went to see the Commodore. Luane was right in the living room with him. And they sure were two damned sick people. I told 'em I didn't see what they had to feel bad about.

"It's the architects' fault," I said. "You've got something pretty new here, in this concealed plumbing, but you ain't got a new-style building to put it in. The architects should have known that with all this angling and turning the water pipes were just about bound to get a vacuum in 'em— Yeah, Commodore?"

"I said," he said, kind of dead-voiced, "that the architects aren't responsible. The blueprints were drawn up from a rough design I made myself. I insisted on having my own way, despite their objections, and they've got a waiver in writing."

I asked him why the hell he'd done it—why pay for expert advice and then not listen to it?

He grimaced, almost crying. "I thought they were trying to run up their bill on me, Pete," he said. "The architect gets six percent of the cost of a job, you know, and since I'm not exactly a trusting person . . ." He broke off, grimacing again. "Not that I've had much reason to trust people. Offhand, I'd say that you were the only completely honest man I've ever met, Pete."

"Well—well, thanks, Commodore," I said. "I—"

"Have you told anyone about this difficulty, Pete? None of the workmen know? Well, do you suppose that if it wasn't corrected—uh—do you suppose the result might be, uh, very serious?"

"I don't know," I said. "Maybe some of the tenants wouldn't be hurt at all. Maybe it might be quite a while before the others came down with anything. I don't know how many might get sick or how many might die, but there's one thing I do know, Commodore. I know I ain't drinking no sewer water myself, and I ain't letting anyone else do it. So—"

I broke off. He was looking so shocked and hurt that I apologized for what I said. Yeah, by God, *I* apologized to *him!*

"Quite all right, Pete," he said. "Your concern for the public welfare is wholly commendable. Now, getting back to our problem, just what if anything can be done about it?"

I told him. The whole building would have to be repiped. Of course, we could use the same piping but it would have to come out of the walls and be put on the outside. What it actually added up to was ripping out the interior of the building, and doing it over again.

"I see." He bit his lip. "What about your men, Pete? How will you explain to them?"

"Well—" I shrugged. "I'll tell 'em I pulled a boner, and I'm making good on it. That won't hurt me none, and they'll be glad to believe it."

"I see," he said again. "Pete—Pete, I have no right to ask it, but everything I have is tied up in that building. Everything! I've exhausted my credit. If I attempt to get any more the building will be plastered with liens from basement to roof. Once it's finished, I'll be in fine shape. The government will lease the ground floor, and I have tenants signed up for most of the offices. But I can't finish it, Pete, unless —and I have no right at all to ask you—"

Luane was sniffling. He put his arm around her, looking at me apologetically, and after a moment she turned and put her arms around him. It seemed pretty pitiful, you know. I took out my notebook and did some figuring.

I didn't have hardly any ready cash, myself, but my credit was first-class. By stretching it right to the limit, I could finance the rework that had to be done, which would probably tot up to about eight thousand dollars.

Well, the Commodore practically wrung my hand off when I told him I'd do it. And I thought for a minute that

Luane was going to kiss me. Then the Commodore gave me his note for ten thousand—ten thousand instead of eight. Because I'd literally saved his and Luane's lives, he said, and even with the two thousand bonus they'd still be eternally in my debt.

Well, I guess I probably don't need to tell you the rest of it, but I'll do it anyway. Just in case you're as dumb as I was.

The Commodore denied that he owed me a red cent for the rework. He said it was due to my own errors, as I'd publicly stated, and that he was contemplating suit against me for failing to follow the architects' specifications.

"Naturally, I'd hate to do it," he said smoothly, sort of smiling down his nose. "I imagine you have quite enough problems, as it is."

I told him that wasn't the only thing I had. I had his note for ten thousand, and I'd collect every penny of it. He shook his head, chuckling.

"I'm afraid not, Pavlov. You see I have no assets; I've transferred everything I owned to my daughter, Luane."

Luane didn't seem too happy about the deal. I looked at her, and she dropped her eyes; and then she turned suddenly to the Commodore.

"Let's not do this, father," she said. "I know you mean it for my benefit, but—"

"Yes," the Commdore nodded. "So the choice is yours. My feeling is that a woman untrained for any work—an unemployable, unmarriageable spinster, to state the case succinctly—is going to need every dollar she can get. But if you feel differently..."

He spread his hands, giving her that down-the-nose smile.

Luane got up and left the room.

I left, too, and I never went back. Because what the hell was the use? I couldn't get anything from her. He didn't have anything to get. He even had me staved off on giving him a beating, him being as old as he was.

So that was that. That was how I made out dealing with

an "old-school gentleman," and a "true aristocrat" and the town's "first citizen" and so on.

It took me five years, working night and day, to get out of debt.

Ralph was sweeping up the dance floor when I got back to the pavilion. I kidded around with him a few minutes, and then I went for a walk down the beach. It was a good walk, sort of—looking at all the things I'd built, and knowing that no one had ever built better. In another way, it wasn't so good: the looking gave me a royal pain. Because I could have collected just as much on cheaper buildings. And if I'd built cheaper, I wouldn't have been in the spot I was in.

I wondered what the hell I'd been thinking about to sink so much dough into seasonal structures. I guessed I hadn't been thinking at all. I'd just done it automatically—building in the only way I knew how to build.

I ran into Mac's singer, Danny Lee, on the beach. She was in a bathing suit, sunning herself, and I sat down by her and talked a while. But not as long as I wanted to. It couldn't do me any good, you know; not just chatting about things in general. And I was afraid if I hung around very long, I might do more than that. Because that little girl, she was the kind that comes few and far between. She was my kind of woman.

That Danny—if she went for you, she'd go all the way. She'd kill for you, even if she knew it might get her killed. You could see it in her. Anyways, I could see it. And it was all wrapped up in such a pretty package.

Well, though, maybe she was my kind of woman, but I wasn't her kind of man. She wouldn't have wanted no part of an old pot-bellied bastard like me, even if she hadn't had Ralph Devore on the string. So I shoved off before I said or did something to make a damned fool of myself.

I circled back toward the pavilion. Rags called to me from his cottage, so I went in and had coffee with him.

He asked me how the money situation was with me, and I

said that it was just about like it had been. He said he was in just about the worst shape he'd ever been in himself.

"Don't know what the hell I'm going to do, Pete. I won't have no band after we close here, and I don't feel like going out single any more. I would, if there was a decent living in it. But it's hard to break even with me on the road and Janie and the boys in New York."

"Yeah," I said, looking down at the floor. Feeling kind of awkward like I always did when he mentioned those boys. "Yeah—uh—I mean, what about recordings, Rags? Can't you get some of them to do?"

He snorted and let out a string of cuss words. He said he wasn't making any more recordings until he was allowed to do the job right. Which would be just about never, unless he owned his own record company.

"I wished you did," I said. "If I was in a little bit better shape, I'd—"

"Yeah, yeah—" He cut me off. "Forget it, Pete. It's really the only damned thing I want to do, but I know it's impossible."

He drained the coffee from his cup, and filled it up with whiskey. He took a sip, smacked his lips and shuddered. After a minute or two, he asked me what I thought about the setup between Danny and Ralph Devore.

"I mean, what can come of it, Pete? How do you think it will wind up?"

I shrugged. I said I guessed I hadn't done much thinking about it.

"I've been wondering," he frowned. "It looks like the real thing between 'em. But that pair—Ralph, in particular— well, they ain't just a couple of lovesick kids. They wouldn't go way out on a limb unless they saw some way off of it."

"No," I said. "I don't figure they would."

"I wonder," he said. "I've been thinking. Y'know, when I first introduced them, I told her he was a rich man. And lately I've been thinking, wouldn't it be a hell of a joke if . . ."

"Yeah?"

"Nothing. What the hell?" he laughed. "Just a crazy notion I had."

"Well, I guess I better be going," I said. "Getting to be about my lunch time."

I headed back into town, and across to the far side. I started to pass by the neighborhood church, and then I slowed down and went back a few steps. I stopped in front of the vacant lot, between the church and the parsonage.

I stood there and stared at it, making myself look thoughtful and interested. Finally, I took a rule out of my pocket, and did a little measuring.

The curtain moved at one of the parsonage windows. I took out a notebook and jotted a few figures into it. Pretended to make some calculations.

I've had a lot of sport with that vacant lot. Once I made out like I'd found some marijuana growing on it, and another time I pretended I was going to buy it for a shooting gallery. What with one stunt and another, I've kept the preacher of that church worried for years. I knew he was peeking through the curtains at me now. Watching and wondering, and working up to another worry-spell.

He came out of the parsonage, finally. He didn't want to, but he just couldn't help it.

I went on with my measuring and figuring, acting like I didn't see him. He hesitated in the yard, and then he came over to the corner of the fence.

"Yes?" he said. "Yes, Mr. Pavlov?"

"Yes," I said. "Yes, sir, I think this will do just fine."

"Fine?" He looked at me water-eyed, his lips starting to tremble. "Mr. Pavlov, what—what do you want of me? I'm an old man, and—"

"Remember when you wasn't," I said. "Remember real well. But talking about this lot here, I was just wondering if it wouldn't be a good spot for a laundry. Though maybe you could throw some business my way."

He knew what I was driving at, all right. No wonder either, after all these years. He looked at me, his eyes watering, his mouth opening and closing. And I told him what I had in mind was the bedsheet business.

"Tell you what I'll do," I said. "You tip off your pals to send their sheets to me, and any patching they need—like buckshot holes, you know—I'll do it for nothing. Probably no more than fair, anyways, since I maybe put 'em there."

"Mr. P-Pavlov," he said. "Can't you ever—?"

"Guess you didn't need many seats in your church for a while, did you?" I said. "Guess most of the fellows didn't feel like settin' down. Not much more like it, maybe, than some of the folks they visited with bullwhips."

I grinned and winked at him. He stood leaning against the fence, his mouth quivering, his hands gripping and ungripping the pickets.

"Mr. Pavlov," he said. "It—that was such a long time ago, Mr. Pavlov."

"Don't seem long to me," I said. "But me, I got a long memory."

"If you know how sorry I was, how often I've begged God's forgiveness . . ."

"Yeah?" I said. "Well, I guess I better be going. I stand around here much longer, I might lose my appetite."

My house was in the next block, a big two-story job with plenty of yard space. It was probably the best-built house in town, but it sure didn't look like much. What it looked like was hell.

I'd been pretty busy at the time I finished it, fifteen years ago. Had four or five contract jobs running—jobs I'd taken money on. Figured I had to take care of them, and do it right, before I prettied up my own place.

So I did that. And while I was doing it, my neighbors hit me with a petition. I tore it up, and threw it at 'em. They took me into court, and I fought 'em to a standstill. If they'd just left me alone, stopped to consider that they didn't have no monopoly on wanting things nice—but they just wouldn't do that. They tried to make me do something. No one makes me do anything.

The house has never been painted. The yard has never

been cleaned up. It's littered with odds and ends of lumber, sawhorses, left-over brick and so on. There's a couple of old wheelbarrows, almost rusted and rotted to bits, and a big mixing trough, caked with cement. There's—

But I already said it.

It looks like hell. It ain't ever going to look any other way—at least, it ain't going to look any better—as long as I'm alive.

It was a couple of minutes after twelve when I went in. So lunch was already on the table, and Myra and my wife, Gretchen, were standing by their chairs waiting for me.

I said hello. They mumbled and ducked their heads. I said, well, let's sit; and we all sat down.

I filled their plates and mine. I took a couple bites—it was beef and potato dumplings—and then I mentioned the matter of Doc Ashton.

"Dug up a big building job for me over in Atlantic Center," I said. "How'd you feel about us all going there to live for four or five months?"

Gretchen didn't look up, but I saw her eyes slant toward Myra. A kind of red flush spread over Myra's face, and her hand shook as she raised her fork.

Halfway to her mouth, the fork slipped out of her fingers, landed with a clatter on her plate. She and Gretchen jumped. I laughed.

"Don't worry," I said. "We ain't going. I never had no notion of going. Just thought I'd tell you about it."

I took a big bite of grub, staring at them while I chewed it. Myra's face got redder and redder. And then she jumped up suddenly, and ran out of the room.

I laughed. I didn't feel much like it, but I did. Gretchen looked up at last.

"Why don't you leave her alone?" she said, not mumbling or whining like she usually does. "Ain't you done enough, taking all the spirit out of her? Beatin' her down until she goes around like a whipped dog? Do you have to go on and on, seeing how miserable—"

"Huh-uh," I said. "That's something I ain't going to do. I sure ain't going on and on."

"What—" She hesitated. "What do you mean by that?"

I shrugged. After a moment or so, she turned and left, headed up the stairs toward Myra's room.

I finished eating, wiping my plate clean with a piece of bread. Afterwards, I dug my teeth a little with a toothpick, and after that I took a big chaw of tobacco. I looked at my watch, then—saw that it was two minutes to one o'clock. I went on looking until the hands pointed to one sharp. Then, I got my hat off the hallrack and started back toward town.

I did everything just like always, you know. Seemed like I hadn't ought to, but I'd never had but one way of doing things, and I stuck to it now. Right or wrong, it was my way. And to me, it seemed right.

Take the spirit out of 'em? Why, hell, I tried to put spirit into 'em! I gave 'em something to be proud of—something to hold their heads high about. I built something out of nothing, just my head and my two bare hands. And I never bent my back to no man while I was doing it. I never let no one take the spirit out of me. And believe me, there was plenty of them that tried. Why, those two—Gretchen and Myra—if they'd taken just half of what I took—

I got back to my office. I finished my chaw, and took a big drink of whiskey. And I kind of laughed to myself and thought, Well, hell. What you got to show for it all, Pieter Pavlovski? A wife? Gretchen's a *wife?* A daughter? Myra— that sheep-eyed slut—is *your* daughter? Well, what then, besides the buildings? *Aside* from your buildings. Because them buildings ain't yours no more. You've held on to them as long as you can, and . . .

I took another big drink. I tried to laugh again, because it was a hell of a joke on me, you know. But I just wasn't up to laughing. Not when it was about losing this pavilion and the hotels and the restaurants and the cottages and—and everything I had. All the things that took the place of what I didn't have.

I couldn't hardly think about it, let alone laugh.

I took the gun out of my desk. I checked it over, and put it back in the drawer again.

I thought, her fault, his fault, theirs, mine, the whole goddamned world's—what the hell's the difference? It's a bad job. It's got your name on it. So there's just one thing to do about it.

It was about nine-thirty when Bobbie Ashton showed up at my office. I'd been drinking quite a bit, and it gave me a pretty bad jar when I looked up and saw him in the doorway. I didn't cuss him out, though—just grunted a "How are you, Bobbie?" and he smiled and sat down.

I said I thought him and Myra were out on a date tonight.

"We were," he nodded. "I mean, we still are. I just drove by to see you for a minute."

"Yeah?" I said. "Wasn't going to ask me if it was all right for you to go with her, was you?"

"No," he said. "I was going to ask if—had you heard that Mrs. Devore was dead?"

"Well, yeah." I sat up a little in my chair. "Ralph called and told me. What about it, anyway?"

"Perhaps nothing," he said. "On the other hand . . ."

He took a long white envelope out of his pocket, and laid it on my desk. He stood up again, smiling a cool, funny little smile.

"I want you to read that," he said. "If it becomes necessary—that is, to protect an innocent person—and you may interpret the word liberally—I want you to use it."

"Use it? What the hell is it?" I said. "Why not use it yourself?"

His smile widened. He shook his head gently. And then, before I could say anything more, he was gone.

I opened the envelope, and began to read.

It was a confession, written in his own handwriting, to the murder of Luane Devore. It told how he'd figured out that Ralph must have had a pile of money saved, and how he needed a pile himself. And it went on to say just how the murder had come about.

He'd had a handkerchief tied over his face. He'd kept quiet—not saying anything, I mean—so she couldn't recognize his voice. He'd slipped upstairs, not intending to really hurt her; just to give her a shove or maybe a sock, so's he could grab the money. And it wasn't his intention to steal it outright. He was going to send it back anonymously as soon as he could. But——well, everything went wrong, and nothing worked out like he'd planned.

Luane was waiting for him at the head of the stairs. She piled into him, and he tried to fight her off. And the next thing he knew, she was lying at the foot of the stairs, dead.

He forgot all about the money, and beat it. He was too scared to do anything else. . . .

I finished reading the confession. I glanced back over it again, kind of marveling over it—wondering how the thing could sound so true unless it was. There was just one hole in it that I could see. That part about him being scared. If it was possible to scare that kid, I didn't know how the hell it would be.

I took another drink. I struck a match to the confession, and tossed it into the spittoon. Because nothing had changed. Killing Luane was one crime he'd never be punished for. And probably he knew it, too.

That was why he'd written the confession—probably. He knew he was going to die anyway, so the confession couldn't hurt him and it might help someone else a lot.

I got my gun out, and slid it into my hip pocket. I turned off the lights and went out to my car.

It was no trouble finding them, Bobbie and Myra. Just a matter of driving a while, and then getting out and walking a while, creeping along a winding trail. All I had to do was think of where I'd go if I was in his place. And the place I'd've gone to was the place he'd taken her.

They were stretched out on a patch of sand in a little clearing, and they were locked together. I couldn't really see her, just him. And that made it pretty hard, because him— he—was all I really cared about.

I didn't know how he'd got to her. Or why. I was afraid to

even think about it, for fear I might try to excuse him. And it couldn't be that way. I was pretty sure he wouldn't want it that way. But it was damned hard, just the same.

Me and him—we were so much alike. We thought so much alike. That was how he'd been able to confess to a killing I'd done—yeah, I killed Luane—and have his facts almost completely straight.

I had planned on sticking Luane up for the money. I had worn a handkerchief over my face, and I hadn't answered when she called downstairs, so that she couldn't recognize my voice.

Then, right at the last minute, I changed my mind; I couldn't go through with the stunt. I'd never pulled anything sneaky in my life, and I couldn't do it now. And, by God, there was no reason why I should.

She owed me money. Ten thousand dollars with almost twenty-five years' interest. I jerked the handkerchief down off my face and put the gun in my pocket, and told her I was there to collect.

"And don't tell me you ain't got it," I said, when she started jabbering and squawking ninety to the minute. "Ralph's made it, and he ain't spent it—and he ain't got it either. You're keeping it to keep him. If Ralph had it, he'd've jumped town with that singer long ago."

I went up the stairs, walking slowly and keeping a sharp eye on her. She begged, and then she began yelling threats. I'd never get away with it, she yelled. She'd have me arrested. I wouldn't get to keep the money, and I'd go to prison besides.

"Maybe," I said, "but I figure not. Everyone thinks I got plenty of money, and even my worst enemy wouldn't never accuse me of stealing. So I figure I'll get away with it. It'll be as easy as it was for you and your Pa to cheat me."

Well, I thought for a minute that she was going to give up. Because she stopped yelling and stood back against the wall, as to let me pass. Then, just as I took the last step, she screamed and lunged at me.

I flung my arm out, trying to ward her off. It caught her a

sweeping blow, and being off balance like she was, she went down the stairs head-first.

I went down and took a quick look at her. I got out of there. I didn't need money no more.

. . . I kind of sighed. I took the gun out of my pocket, staring across to the patch of sand where Bobbie and Myra were.

I hesitated, wondering if I ought to toss a rock at them. Give 'em a chance, you know, like you do when you're out hunting and you see a setting rabbit.

But they weren't rabbits. He wasn't, anyway. And if I didn't get them now, I'd just have to do the job later. And there wasn't going to be any later for me. I wouldn't be roaming around after tonight. So I raised the gun and took aim.

I waited a second. Two or three seconds. He turned his head suddenly, and kissed her. And, then, right at that moment, I started shooting.

I figure they died happy.

I blew the smoke out of my gun, went back to my car and headed for town. I drove to the courthouse and turned myself in for the three killings.

Kossy was my lawyer at the trial. But there wasn't nothing a lawyer could do for me. There wasn't nothing I'd've let him do. So now it's all over—or it damned soon will be—and now that it is, I kind of wonder.

I wonder if I really did kill Luane Devore.

She was a pretty tough old bag. Could be that the fall downstairs just knocked her out, and someone else came along and finished the job. Could be that someone was hiding in the house right at the time I was there.

It would be just about a perfect murder, you know. They, this party, could do the killing and I'd take the blame for it. Anyone who knew me knew that I would.

Who do I think did it—that is, if I didn't?

Well, I don't figure it was anyone you might ordinarily suspect, the people who seemed to have the best motives. The very fact that they had good reasons for wanting Luane dead—and that everyone knew it—would be the thing that would keep them from killing her. They'd be too afraid, you know, that the job might be pinned on them.

Aside from that, and maybe excepting Danny Lee, all the prime suspects were too fond of living to commit murder. They'd proved it over and over, through the years; proved it by the way they lived. They'd give up their principles, their good name—everything they had; just as long as they could go on living. Living any damned old way. And people like that, they ain't going to take the risk of killing.

Me, now, I'm not that way—just in case you haven't discovered it. I have to live a certain way or I'd rather be dead, which I'm just about to be. Putting it in a nutshell, I never had but one thing to live for. And if I thought I was going to lose that, like I did lose it, why...

I guess you see what I'm driving at. Whoever killed Luane was a one-reason-for-living person. Whoever killed Luane was someone who didn't seem to have a motive—who could do it with a good chance of never being suspected. And there's only one person I can think of who fits that description.

She was smart and efficient, but she'd stuck to the same cheap dull job for years. She was pretty as a picture and a damned nice girl to boot, but she'd never gotten married.

She stuck to her job and she'd never gotten married for the same reason—because she was in love with her boss. She never showed it in any of the usual ways. She never made any passes at him—she wasn't that kind. And she never stepped out with him. There wasn't a thing she did that could cause gossip about her. But, hell, it was plain as day how she felt. It was clear to me, anyway. I'd seen the way she kowtowed to him, and made over him, and it kind of made me squirm. I'd think: Now, why the hell does she do it—a gal that could have her pick of jobs and men? And of course there couldn't be but one reason why she did it.

She must have known that he was nothing but a fat-mouthed dunce. She must have known that he wasn't ever going to marry her—that he was too self-centered to marry anyone, and that his sister wouldn't let him if he wanted to. But that didn't change anything. Maybe, women being like they are, it might have made her love him all the more. Anyway, she was crazy about him—she *had* to be, you know—crazy enough to kill anyone who hurt him. And someone was hurting him. It was getting to the point where he might lose his job—the only one he could hold—and if he did they'd be separated, and—

Yeah, that's right. I'm talking about Nellie Otis, the county attorney's secretary.

I figure that Nellie killed Luane—if I didn't do it. I guess I ain't ever likely to know for sure, and I don't know as I give a damn.

I was just wondering, you know, thinking. And now that I've thought it through, to hell with it.

MORE MYSTERIOUS PLEASURES

HAROLD ADAMS
MURDER
Carl Wilcox debuts in a story of triple murder which exposes the underbelly of corruption in the town of Corden, shattering the respectability of its most dignified citizens.   **#501 $3.50**

THE NAKED LIAR
When a sexy young widow is framed for the murder of her husband, Carl Wilcox comes through to help her fight off cops and big-city goons.   **#420 $3.95**

THE FOURTH WIDOW
Ex-con/private eye Carl Wilcox is back, investigating the death of a "popular" widow in the Depression-era town of Corden, S.D.   **#502 $3.50**

EARL DERR BIGGERS
THE HOUSE WITHOUT A KEY
Charlie Chan debuts in the Honolulu investigation of an expatriate Bostonian's murder.   **#421 $3.95**

THE CHINESE PARROT
Charlie Chan works to find the key to murders seemingly without victims—but which have left a multitude of clues.   **#503 $3.95**

BEHIND THAT CURTAIN
Two murders sixteen years apart, one in London, one in San Francisco, each share a major clue in a pair of velvet Chinese slippers. Chan seeks the connection.   **#504 $3.95**

THE BLACK CAMEL
When movie goddess Sheila Fane is murdered in her Hawaiian pavilion, Chan discovers an interrelated crime in a murky Hollywood mystery from the past.   **#505 $3.95**

CHARLIE CHAN CARRIES ON
An elusive transcontinental killer dogs the heels of the Lofton Round the World Cruise. When the touring party reaches Honolulu, the murderer finally meets his match.   **#506 $3.95**

DAVID WILLIAMS' "MARK TREASURE" SERIES
UNHOLY WRIT
London financier Mark Treasure helps a friend reacquire some property. He stays to unravel the mystery when a Shakespeare manuscript is discovered and foul murder done. #112 $3.95

TREASURE BY DEGREES
Mark Treasure discovers there's nothing funny about a board game called "Funny Farms." When he becomes involved in the takeover struggle for a small university, he also finds there's nothing funny about murder. #113 $3.95

■ ■

AVAILABLE AT YOUR BOOKSTORE OR DIRECT FROM THE PUBLISHER

Mysterious Press Mail Order
129 West 56th Street
New York, NY 10019

Please send me the MYSTERIOUS PRESS titles I have circled below:

103 105 106 107 112 113 208 209 210 211 212 213
214 215 216 217 218 219 220 301 302 303 304 305
306 308 309 315 316 401 402 403 404 405 406 407
408 409 410 411 412 413 414 415 416 417 418 419
420 421 501 502 503 504 505 506 507 508 509 510
511 512 513 514 515 516 517 518 519 520 521 522
523 524 525 526 527 528 529 530 531 532 533 534
535 536 537 538 539 540 541 542 543 544 545

I am enclosing $ _____ (please add $2.00 postage and handling for the first book, and 25¢ for each additional book). Send check or money order only—no cash or C.O.D.'s please. Allow at least 4 weeks for delivery.

NAME _____

ADDRESS _____

CITY _____ STATE _____ ZIP CODE _____
New York State residents please add appropriate sales tax.